Heck Carson Series Volume 5

by

John Spiars

Forgotten Country John Spiars

Version 1.0 – October, 2018

Published by Under the Lone Star Books

ISBN: 9781729355787

Copyright © 2018 by John Spiars

Discover other titles by John Spiars and read his monthly blog at
www.underthelonestar.com

This book is a work of fiction. Names, characters, places and incidents either are products of the author's imagination or are used fictitiously. Any resemblance to actual events or locales or persons, living or dead, is entirely coincidental.

All rights reserved, including the right of reproduction in whole or in part in any form.

TABLE OF CONTENTS

TABLE OF CONTENTS 3
CHAPTER ONE 5
CHAPTER TWO 9
CHAPTER THREE..................16
CHAPTER FOUR 28
CHAPTER FIVE 36
CHAPTER SIX 43
CHAPTER SEVEN 48
CHAPTER EIGHT...................57
CHAPTER NINE......................64
CHAPTER TEN.......................71
CHAPTER ELEVEN 77
CHAPTER TWELVE 83
CHAPTER THIRTEEN..........94
CHAPTER FOURTEEN.........105
CHAPTER FIFTEEN 111
CHAPTER SIXTEEN 117
CHAPTER SEVENTEEN.......124
CHAPTER EIGHTEEN 130
CHAPTER NINETEEN..........136
CHAPTER TWENTY 144
CHAPTER TWENTY-ONE ...150
CHAPTER TWENTY-TWO..156
CHAPTER TWENTY-THREE...167
CHAPTER TWENTY-FOUR 176
CHAPTER TWENTY-FIVE ..185
CHAPTER TWENTY-SIX 189
CHAPTER TWENTY-SEVEN…196
CHAPTER TWENTY-EIGHT…203
CHAPTER TWENTY-NINE..209

CHAPTER THIRTY 219
CHAPTER THIRTY-ONE 225
CHAPTER THIRTY-TWO 231
CHAPTER THIRTY-THREE 236
CHAPTER THIRTY-FOUR .. 245
CHAPTER THIRTY-FIVE 249
CHAPTER THIRTY-SIX 255
ABOUT THE AUTHOR 259
OTHER BOOKS BY JOHN SPIARS ... 260

Chapter One

"Are ya gonna get them shingles on the roof, or can we take the rest of the day off? I've gotta fresh jug waiting for me if we're done."

"The whiskey can wait, Ulley. We need to get that roof fixed, cause I'm tired of waking up soaked every time it rains," Darby said, heaving a stack of wood shingles up to the roof.

"Darby, you ain't getting in the spirit of things," Ulley said. "Heck just doesn't want you to miss that horse stall you used to live in."

"When y'all are done yapping," Heck said, "maybe ya could give me a hand. I'd like to get to some work that will actually make us money, but I can't do that till this roof is fixed."

"I'm glad to hear that, cause it's been Darby and me doing all the work around here while you traipse around the state playing bounty hunter."

As he reached down to grab another bundle of shingles, Heck looked out over the rolling grasslands that made up his ranch. He stared past the herd of grazing cattle and gazed at the gently flowing waters of the Brazos River. It had been a hard road, it still was in most ways, but his dream was finally coming into focus. Although he had to admit, Ulley was right. He'd been so busy working for Governor Davis that he hadn't been able to put in much work on his dream. If it hadn't been for Ulley and Darby, they would still be sleeping under the stars in the middle of the desolate wilderness.

After driving nails for a few more hours, the sun disappeared below the purple horizon, and it became too dark to see.

"I reckon it's about time to call it a day," Heck said, throwing his hammer to the ground, barely missing Ulley's right foot. "What's for supper?"

Picking up the hammer, Ulley thought for a moment about throwing it at Heck's head, but instead he let it drop back to the ground. "We've been partners for three years, and I ain't cooked you a meal yet. Until you hire us a cook, what's for supper is you and Darby's problem. If we're done working for the day, then I got a jug calling my name."

"Don't you ever eat?" Darby asked, as he climbed down the rickety wooden ladder.

"Corn squeezin's have got everything I need. Now, if it's all the same to you, I'll bid you both good night."

CHAPTER TWO

A day and a half out of Fort Worth, Heck and Darby steamed across the state towards El Paso. As the train bounced and rolled along the tracks, Heck hoped his back would survive the trip. The wooden seats allowed precious little in the way of comfort, but he had to admit, it beat spending a month in the saddle.

"What's your plan once we reach El Paso?" Darby asked, trying to pass the time by drawing Heck into conversation. He had worked for him for almost three years, but he still found the man's quiet nature more than a little unsettling.

"We won't get much help from the local law, so I figure we'd ask around at the saloons and gambling houses. One way or another, that should shake 'em loose."

"That sounds like a good way to get ourselves killed," Darby said nervously.

"I hope it don't come to that," Heck said with a smile, "but that shouldn't worry an experienced lawman like you."

Darby took a deep breath and looked at the floor. "I never told ya why I stopped wearing the badge, did I?"

"No, you didn't, but I figured it wasn't any of my business."

"It ain't really much of a story. One day I walked into a saloon to stop a brawl, but it was just put on to lure me in. I hadn't taken more than a couple of steps inside, when someone shot me in the back. I spent three weeks between life and death, and by the time I was back on my feet, I just couldn't bring myself to pin the badge back on."

Darby's story hit home with Heck, and he was reminded of his own time spent clinging to life after being shot in the back.

"That was some bad luck and would certainly make a man reconsider his situation," Heck replied, doing his best to offer a sympathetic ear to Darby, while at the same time trying to gird the young man's courage for what was likely to come.

"Hell, Heck, what kind of man do ya think I am? It weren't the getting shot, but the fact that none of my fellow citizens turned over the man who shot me."

"Yeah, that's certainly worse than just getting shot. What did ya do after that?"

Staring back at his feet, Darby hesitated to answer Heck's question. Heck noticed the young man's discomfort and decided to let him off the hook.

"You don't have to tell me if you'd rather not, but it was you that wanted to pass the time with conversation."

Raising his head, Darby cracked a half-hearted smile and said, "I drifted for a few years, trying to find work where I could, but being a lawman was all I knew. When you found me sleeping in that horse stall, I was at the end of my rope. I'd taken to eating scraps out of ash cans and was at the point of giving up, but you saved me. I don't think I ever thanked you for that."

Heck dismissed the suggestion that he had done anything so noble. He was a practical man and didn't see the need to attach any Christian charity to his motives. "You give me a hard day's work in exchange for your wages and there's no need to make any more of things than that. It looks like we're fixing to pull into a station. Let's see if we can find us something to eat."

As the two men stepped onto the empty train platform, a strong north wind kicked up a cloud of dust from the street, and Heck buttoned up his black frock coat in an effort to stave off the cold that had already chilled him to the bone.

A short walk across the street brought Heck and Darby to the town's café, the sort of place that catered mainly to the locals, and where strangers were apt to receive curious stares from the patrons.

"It'll feel good to get indoors," Darby said, pushing against the wind to close the door. "That cold and dirt is about to beat me to pieces."

"That wind is brutal for sure," Heck said, as he walked past the icy stares of the customers.

They took a table in the back of the café that offered a view of the whole room and a perfect line of sight to the door. Heck sat in a chair so that he could keep the wall to his back and loosened his Colt in its holster. It was a routine that had taken him a while to learn, but one which had now become second nature, though he hoped to see the day when it would no longer be necessary.

The two men weren't seated long before a middle-aged woman approached their table, though the expression on her face was not one of hospitality.

"What do you men want?" she asked coldly.

"We just want breakfast," Heck said, puzzled by the woman's rudeness.

"We don't like gunmen in our town, and I don't like trash in my place. I would prefer you two found another place to eat, but if ya insist on staying, please eat quick and move along."

"Like my friend said, we just want breakfast. We certainly don't want any trouble," Darby said.

"Men like you always say you don't want trouble, but it follows you just the same."

"Ma'am, we just got off the train, and in an hour we'll be getting back on it, but in the meantime, we would like some breakfast," Heck said.

"You heard what the lady said, we don't want your kind in our town." The man speaking was a well-dressed gentleman and was obviously someone of importance. Behind him were three other men, who were undoubtedly used to taking orders from him, and all four were wearing pistols. A fifth man covered the door.

"Howdy, gents," Darby said with a smile. "We seem to have a misunderstanding here. I am Darby Mills and my companion is Heck Carson, a former Ranger. We are traveling to El Paso on important business for the governor."

"My name is Isaiah Cooper, and this is my town. I don't bow down to no governor appointed by the Yankees and I don't like bounty hunters any better than I like gun fighters. If y'all come along quietly, we might just run you out of town with a few bruises."

"That's a mighty generous offer, Mister Cooper, but I'm afraid we just don't have the time to enjoy your hospitality."

Jumping to his feet, Heck tackled Isaiah Cooper, and pulling his Bowie knife, he brought its stag handle down on the side of the man's head.

As Heck made his move, Darby made his. With the butt of his pistol, he laid two of Cooper's men out on the floor. The third man pulled his pistol, but Heck was faster. A bullet to the man's knee caused him to drop like a stone.

"You at the door," Heck yelled. "Unless you want me to end your boss, you'd better drop your gun and let us pass."

The man at the door, favoring his job over the chance to kill the two strangers, quickly dropped his pistol and moved away from the door.

Grabbing the men's guns, Heck and Darby walked into the street.

"It looks like we'll have to travel a little further on empty stomachs," Heck said, as the two made their way to the train station.

"We may get a chance to eat sooner than ya think," Darby said, pointing to a group of men approaching from their left, "but it looks like we might be taking our meals from the city jail."

There were four men, each carrying a coach gun, and with a badge pinned to the front of their shirts.

"Hold it right there, boys," the sheriff said, over the sound of a train whistle. "I've got enough fire power here to blast you two into eternity, but I'd rather just escort y'all to our town's jail."

With his hands raised high in the air, Heck walked towards the sheriff. "I'm sorry about the mess at the café, but we had a bit of a misunderstanding with your Mister Cooper."

"Kill him, did ya?" the sheriff asked, without the least bit of concern in his voice.

"I don't know why your town has us pegged as killers, but we ain't. We are, as it happens, in the employ of Governor Davis. This telegraph should explain everything."

Heck carefully handed the sheriff the telegraph from the governor as the deputies leveled their shotguns at his head.

The sheriff took several minutes to look over the paper, and then instructed his men to lower their weapons.

"I'm sorry, Mister Carson, but since reconstruction, our town has constantly been under attack from the most vile and ruthless outlaws. Mister Cooper and his men have taken it into their mind to head off any trouble before it starts. Their methods have helped to keep us safe, but I'm afraid it has also led to a few innocent people paying the price."

"You're the law around here, so these are matters best left to you. As for me and Darby, well we're no worse for wear, but I'm afraid Cooper and his men will be needing some time to heal."

The sheriff laughed at the thought of Isaiah Cooper being laid up for a few days. "I'm sure it's no less than he deserves, and I'm sorry for all the trouble he caused ya."

"Thank ya, sheriff. If there's nothing else, we'd better get moving before our train leaves without us."

"Go with our blessing," the sheriff said, shaking Heck's hand. "You've got a reputation for being a good lawman, and I figure you've done a lot more for Texas than men like Cooper."

"Thank you, sheriff," Heck said, directing Darby toward their waiting train.

Chapter Three

After several more uncomfortable days traveling through the rugged West Texas desert, the Texas Limited finally pulled into the El Paso depot.

Stepping off the platform, the two men weaved their way between the wagons, carriages, and scores of people on horseback.

"How are we supposed to find two men among all of these people?" Darby asked, as they narrowly avoided being run down by an unobservant freight driver. "It's unlikely that the law would have noticed two strangers in town."

"We'll want to avoid any dealings with the sheriff. Our best bet is to start looking in the saloons and brothels, and we'll also try to sniff out the local bad men. The Vega brothers won't be found among the decent folks, but with other killers and thieves."

"That makes sense," Darby said, "but why do we need to stay away from the law?"

Pulling Darby close, Heck whispered, "Let's just say that the sheriff has a lot more in common with the thieves and killers around here than he does with the law-abiding citizens. With any luck, we'll find the men we're looking for and be outta here before the sheriff even knows we were in town."

"I'm new to all this, but I'd bet that things never go that easy," Darby said.

"You'd be right about that, but a body can always hope," Heck said, as the two men stepped through the doors of a saloon.

One hour and three saloons later, Heck and Darby still hadn't found the men they were looking for, but Darby had found that he wasn't walking quite as steady as he had been.

"I hope we find these outlaws soon," Darby said, "cause if we have to visit many more saloons, I won't be able to stand."

Shaking his head, Heck said, "That's why I've been sticking to beer. I said to look natural, but I never told ya to drink whiskey."

"I'll keep that in mind," Darby said. "Where's our next stop?"

"There's a cantina at the end of the street. The man that owns it ain't exactly above board, but for a few dollars, he can be very agreeable."

Walking through the bat-wing doors of the cantina, Heck and Darby were once again the object of sinister stares and whispered conversation.

Sitting around the dozen or so tables were an assortment of vaqueros, Comancheros, and mercenaries. They peered at the two men from under their wide-brimmed sombreros, and Darby imagined that they were plotting the two men's demise.

Darby followed Heck toward the back of the cantina, nervously turning his head in every direction as he expected to be set on by the whole crowd at any moment. "These fellers don't seem too friendly. What are the chances they might shoot us in the back?"

"Don't worry," Heck replied. "They would never shoot us in the back. This crowd would never let their enemies off that easy."

"That don't give me much comfort, Heck."

"These men are all wanted by the law, so if they find out we're tracking a couple of outlaws, they'll kill us in the most painful way they can. They also don't cotton to gringos much, so stay on your toes and be ready for anything."

Heck's warning only served to make Darby even more nervous than before, and he desperately tried to push away the feeling to make a run for the door.

"So, what about this friend of yours, the owner of this fine establishment?"

"I'd hardly call him a friend," Heck said, "but he makes a tidy sum selling information, so if he's seen the Vega brothers, chances are good he'll tell us, for a price of course."

Stepping up to the long, dusty bar, Heck waved the barkeeper over and ordered two beers. The small Mexican man behind the bar seemed less than eager to wait on the two strangers, but begrudgingly, he drew two beers and slammed the foamy mugs down in front of them.

"Thank you," Heck said, placing several coins down on the bar. "Is there any chance I could talk to Fernando?"

Eyeing the two suspiciously, the barkeeper took a moment and then nodded his head.

After only a few minutes, the barkeep returned and led Heck to a backroom, but Darby was instructed to wait at the bar.

Seated at a table in the small room behind the bar, three men were enjoying a game of cards and a bottle of tequila. The three seemed to be taking more pleasure in the bottle than the game, and Heck doubted whether any of them could stand without grabbing on to something for balance.

Heck hadn't seen the man in years, but he recognized Fernando immediately. He was a fat slob of a man, whose appetite for food and money was exceeded only by his vicious and lazy nature.

"Heck Carson, my old friend, how long has it been?" Fernando said, in nearly perfect English.

Heck walked to the middle of the room where he could keep an eye on all three, just in case Fernando wasn't in a mood to deal. "It's been years, but I don't recall us ever being friends."

"What kind of way is that to talk? Have I not always helped when you've come to me for assistance?"

Heck was only half listening to what Fernando was saying as he kept a wary eye on the other two men. Their dress was decidedly American, but Heck could see that their pistols sat in hand-tooled holsters adorned in the

Mexican style and the boots the two men wore were the type preferred by vaqueros.

"Mister Carson," Fernando repeated, "Have I not always been willing whenever you have come to me for help?"

"Yes," Heck answered, "and you've always been paid well for your assistance. You'll be paid well this time too, if you can help me locate the men I'm looking for."

"You hurt me, Señor," Fernando said, stumbling to his feet. "I am not so in love with money that I would allow it to come between our friendship. I will happily tell you where to find the Vega brothers, and it will cost you nothing."

Fernando shuffled across the room, occasionally steadying himself as he swayed from side to side. From the top of his desk, he retrieved another glass.

"How do you know I came here for the Vega brothers?" Heck asked, keeping his eye on the men seated at the table. "I never told you who I was looking for."

"Señor, everyone who comes to El Paso has a secret, and it is my business to learn what they are. Now, have a drink while we talk over our business."

Heck waved off the glass that Fernando offered and said, "I don't want a drink, and the only business we have is for you to tell me where to find the men I seek. You do know where I can find them, don't ya?"

"Of course, I do. They are right here," Fernando said, indicating the two men seated at the table.

Before Fernando or the Vega brothers knew what was happening, Heck's pistol was in his hand and pointed at the closest Vega brother.

"Luis and Benito, I have warrants for your arrest sworn out by the governor, and I'll be delivering y'all to the United States Marshal in Fort Hancock. Fernando, I'm sure the marshal will be interested to know why two wanted killers were found hiding in your establishment."

"Señor Carson, you are making this more difficult than it has to be. I had hoped we could have a drink and work out a civilized answer to our problem. I would have even offered to pay you for just riding out of town, but now, I'm afraid you will not be leaving here alive."

The two Vega brothers remained still and silent as Heck continued to cover them with his pistol. He glanced at Fernando, who was sipping his tequila as though he was passing the time with an old friend. "You're awfully sure of yourself for someone looking down the wrong end of a Peacemaker."

Fernando smiled at Heck and set his empty glass on the table. "Señor, you may have me and my two friends at the disadvantage, but my man at the bar has a shotgun pointed at your friend's head. If I don't get out there to stop him, he will pull the trigger."

Heck stepped back toward the door and peered through the opening. It was just like Fernando had promised, the barkeep had a shotgun pointed at Darby.

"If your man kills him, I will put a bullet in each of you long before any of your people make it in here to help ya."

Fernando laughed, like Heck's words were the funniest ones he had ever heard. "I have no doubt that is true, but I know men, and I'm betting you're not willing to sacrifice your friend just to deliver two killers to the marshal. I would be willing to do that, but not you."

Heck thought about calling the fat man's bluff, but he knew the cantina owner was right. He wasn't about to take the chance that Darby might be killed.

Forgotten Country   John Spiars

As he contemplated his situation, the words of Jim King came back to him. "Keep those you care about at arm's length. They will just get in your way and make it harder to do your job."

Heck uncocked his pistol and reluctantly handed it to Fernando, who accepted it with the self-satisfying smirk of one who knew exactly how things would play out.

"That was a very wise decision, Señor Carson. You and your young friend will still die, but I might be willing to show you some mercy and make your death quick."

"Me and my brother do not want an easy death for this gringo," Luis Vega said, turning to face Heck for the first time. "He has interfered with our business, and for that, he must suffer."

"Don't tell me how to handle things in my town," Fernando snapped. "I will deal with this nuisance and then you and your brother will be free to steal all of the horses you wish, as long as I receive my cut, of course. Now, if you'll go back to the hotel, I will deal with this."

With his own pistol pointed at his back, Heck was led into the cantina by Fernando. Darby was still being covered by the barkeeper's shotgun, as well as several more of Fernando's men.

"Hey, Heck," Darby said cheerfully. "This friend of yours sure has a strange sense of hospitality."

"I wish everyone would stop calling him that. He's a snake, and any friends he had, he probably shot in the back long ago."

"That's not a very nice thing to say to a man who holds your life in his hands," Fernando said, striking Heck in the back with the barrel of his Colt. The blow drove Heck to his knees and while it hurt considerably, it also provided the opportunity he was looking for.

Grabbing Fernando by the leg, Heck pulled the big man off his feet, and grabbed the Colt from his hands.

A large chunk of floor close to Heck's head was blown to pieces by a blast from the barkeeper's shotgun, but a well-placed shot from Heck's gun kept him from firing the second barrel.

Diving over the bar, Darby barely avoided being cut down by Fernando's other men. He pulled the shotgun from the barkeep's lifeless hands and retrieved his Remington from the man's belt.

After saying a quick prayer, Darby jumped to his feet and dropped the first man he saw with a shotgun blast to the chest. He then sent another of Fernando's men to his grave with a quick shot from his pistol before ducking back behind the bar.

With numerous shots striking the floor around his head and feet, Heck managed to jump up and make it to cover behind an overturned table. From behind the table, Heck saw that Darby had managed to take down two of Fernando's killers, and he figured it was time he did his share as well.

Seizing his chance to make it out of the line of fire, and not one to pass on a chance to save his own skin, Fernando made a run for his office. He might have made it to safety, had he not stopped to fire at Heck, or if he had been a quicker shot. As it was, he just made an easy target, and died a painful death with a bullet lodged in his lung.

Seeing their boss's blood staining the floor caused the last two gunmen to freeze in shock, as the remaining customers ran for the door.

Heck and Darby both rose to their feet and began firing at the two men until both were down and no longer moving.

"You okay, Heck?" Darby yelled, in the now silent cantina, his ears still ringing from the gunfire.

"Yeah, I reckon I'll make it. How about you?"

"I'm good," he shouted back, "but it was touch and go there for a minute."

"I'm glad, but you ain't gotta shout."

"Sorry," Darby said. "My ears ain't working so good after all the shooting."

Heck ejected the empty shells from his pistol and began thumbing in new bullets as he walked towards the back door. "We'd better get outta here before the marshal shows up. Fernando paid him a lot of money and he won't be happy to see we killed his benefactor. Besides, if we hurry, we might still be able to capture the Vega brothers before they leave town."

After two hours of searching hotels and evading the marshal's men, Heck and Darby were able to corner Benito Vega in a livery stable.

"You might as well come on out," Heck called from the door of the livery. "If we have to come in and get ya, there's liable to be bloodshed."

After only a few seconds, Benito recognized the wisdom of Heck's words. "Okay, I'm coming out. My gun's in my holster, so don't shoot."

"You made the right decision, Benito, but where is your brother?" Heck asked, as he searched his prisoner.

"He said he was going back to New Mexico. Luis talks big, but he is too full of fear. He was willing to leave all the horses we worked so hard to steal, but I am not one to give up so easy. It seems I am the bigger fool."

"Some might say I'm the biggest fool of all for coming all this way after ya, but I don't reckon any of that really matters."

"What do we do now?" Darby asked, as he looked up and down the empty street. "If that crooked marshal finds us, we'll all hang."

"We get our horses and deliver our prisoner to Fort Hancock. From there, I'll set out for New Mexico and you'll head for my brother's ranch to prepare for our drive."

The two men rode day and night through the harsh West Texas desert, escorting their prisoner to his date with justice. A day and a half of hard riding brought the men into the city limits of Fort Hancock, which was the closest town with a lawman who was not controlled by the horse and cattle thieves who held the real power along the border.

"I hope the sheriff in this town is better than the law back in El Paso," Darby said, as they dismounted in front of the sheriff's office.

"Sheriff Campbell keeps order in one of the most violent parts of Texas, so he has to be hard and at times ruthless, but he's an honest lawman."

"Those are some mighty nice words, Ranger Carson, but they won't keep me from locking you up if ya cause any trouble in my town," the sheriff said, stepping through the door of the jail.

"Pat Campbell, I'm glad to see old age ain't hurt your hearing none," Heck said, walking over to greet his old friend.

"Old? I can still best you in a scrape and don't you forget it. Now, why don't ya introduce me to your friends."

"This fella here is Darby Mills. He works for me on my ranch. The other man is Benito Vega. He's an outlaw we planned on leaving with ya. I've got paper on him, so I'd be obliged if you'd wire the governor and let him know I delivered him."

"Good to meet ya, Darby," Sheriff Campbell said, extending his hand. "Let's get this outlaw locked up and get y'all over to the café for supper. Darby, I'll tell the cook to bring ya extra, cause if you're working for Heck, I'm sure you don't get to eat regular."

"Dang, Heck," Darby said, "this man knows ya pretty good."

Over heaping plates of fried meat, frijoles, and tortillas, Sheriff Campbell regaled Darby with stories of how Heck and the other Rangers from Company C helped him run out the bad element that had once ruled over Fort Hancock.

"I tell ya Darby, I ain't never seen nothing like it. Folks say I'm rough, but I don't have nothing on Heck Carson. We had a street full of desperados that would have made the devil himself turn tail, and there was Ranger Carson right out there in the middle of 'em, a pistol in each hand, daring 'em to do their worst."

"Don't believe everything this man says," Heck said, concentrating more on his dinner than the conversation. "It wasn't as bad as he makes out."

"All I know is the fighting went on for two days and nights, and when the smoke finally cleared, the only ones still moving on the street was me and the boys of Company C," the sheriff said, dismissing Heck's false modesty.

"I know one thing," Heck said, "I'll be glad to hit the trail by myself for a while, there's too much useless talk around here."

"I'm glad to see that you're still the same mean cuss you always was."

"Ya really going after Luis Vega by yourself?" Darby asked, between bites of tortilla.

"I don't have a choice. The governor ordered me to bring in both brothers, so I gotta catch up to him before he has a mind to slip down into Mexico. Besides, between the two of 'em, Luis is the one more in need of a hanging."

"I still say you should let me go with ya, especially if he's as bad as you say."

"You've gotta get to my brother's ranch and help him prepare the herd for us to drive them north. If we don't get those cows and horses to our ranch, we won't have enough to drive to market next year."

"I told ya, sonny. Heck may shy away from the stories, but he don't mind building the legend," Sheriff Campbell said, needling his old friend.

"Say what ya will," Heck replied, "but I've got a job to do and I ain't gonna quit till it's done."

"Just be careful. New Mexico ain't what it used to be. They got these vigilance committees there now, and them boys don't cotton much to outsiders coming in to administer law. They've killed more people than consumption, and half of them have been lawmen who got in their way."

"I'll be as careful as I can be."

Chapter Four

Heck once again rode west, though this time he gave El Paso a wide birth. He followed the Rio Grande and crossed the rugged, reddish colored mountains into New Mexico Territory. He made his way across the empty desert at night, and during the day he slept in rocky outcroppings that offered protection from the deadly rays of the sun. Even with these precautions, Heck's face and lips were blistered, and he found himself drinking much more water than usual. Heck chose to follow the Rio Grande, not only because it provided a continuous source of water, but because he was sure Luis Vega would have chosen to stick to the river, at least for a while. He hoped that Vega might figure he'd gotten away and choose to stop for a day or two to rest, and perhaps he might get lucky and catch the horse thief napping.

Forgotten Country — John Spiars

Knowing that with Vega's head start it would be hard to catch up to him, Heck chose to snack on apples, so he wouldn't have to stop so often to water himself and his horse. They provided much needed moisture as well as nourishment, though after a few days he would have gladly traded them for a nice beef steak and fried potatoes.

When not eating or sleeping, he ventured into the heat for a few minutes each day to scout Vega's trail, and assure himself he was still heading in the right direction. From the freshness of the tracks, Heck could tell that his prey was still at least five days ahead of him, and he knew there was little chance he would catch up to Luis anytime soon. The only advantage Heck had was that his enemy had no idea he was being pursued and he hoped overconfidence would prompt Vega to hole up at some point. Heck figured that he would be looking for the closest opportunity to kick up his heels and possibly engage in a little horse or cattle theft. If he was right, that would mean Luis Vega was likely headed for Santa Fe.

Traveling by night made the going slow, even with a three quarters moon providing light by which to see; each step had to be carefully measured. In the rocky terrain, one misstep could cause him to be thrown from his horse, or worse, his horse could fall and break a leg, leaving Heck to make the rest of his journey on foot. He was not by nature a patient man, but his experience traveling in harsh conditions kept his natural instincts in check. Impatience and foolishness had killed more men than Indians and outlaws combined, and Heck had no interest in having his tombstone saying he'd died by falling from his horse.

Slowly, the terrain changed from inhospitable desert to rolling hills of lush grasslands. Once in the high country, Heck took the opportunity to let his horse graze on the green grass, while he took a day to rest in the cooler temperatures of northern New Mexico. While resting, Heck built a rabbit snare and enjoyed the first meat he had eaten in over a week, which helped to strengthen his body, but more importantly, it buoyed his spirits for his final push to Santa Fe.

He could finally see the end of his latest crusade, but his exuberance was tempered by the knowledge that Luis Vega might have already moved on from Santa Fe by the time he arrived there. If that happened, as much as he would hate to, Heck would be forced to abandon his pursuit. Jefferson and Darby would have the cattle and horses ready to move north before long, and the drive couldn't be put off, no matter how many outlaws needed capturing. Not a man given to worrying about things he couldn't change, he quickly put these negative thoughts out of his mind and laid down on the carpet of soft grass, secure in the belief that God had not led him so far only to allow his prey to slip through his grasp.

It was this same faith that made him certain he would be a success as a rancher. His whole life was about to culminate in his ultimate dream of building something great, of helping to lead Texas into the next century. All the battles he had survived and the wars he had participated in, were all leading him to something greater, and the only battle left to fight was a few miles away in Santa Fe. Once he collected the bounty on the Vega brothers, he would have enough money to support the ranch for the next year.

Santa Fe was bustling with activity as Heck rode into town, and he was carried along the busy street by a sea of rowdy cowboys, traders, shoppers and those just seeking a good time. The noise caused by the herds of revelers was a stark contrast to the weeks of silent contemplation that Heck had grown used to, and it took some minutes before he was able to adjust and concentrate on his search. Even after shaking the cobwebs loose, picking out one man among the hundreds moving along the crowded street seemed to be an impossible task.

Heck didn't bother renting a room, as he hoped to find Luis Vega quickly and then rush him out of town under cover of darkness. Judging from the crowds, he doubted there would have been any rooms available anyway, even if he had been inclined to spend the night.

The adobe buildings were low set and held together with thick oak beams, in typical Spanish fashion. They were set close together and connected by the wooden boardwalks which allowed the patrons to move from place to place without having to slog through the muddy streets during the rainy months. As with most towns that catered to the cattle trade, the main business in Santa Fe was vice, and throngs of young men pushed their way through the open doors, eager to surrender the money they had spent months earning.

In his younger days, Heck and his Ranger companions would have been the first ones to lay their money down, but now he was more interested in being the one bringing the money in. After a life of adventure, danger, and howling at the moon, it seemed much more appealing to build something of substance, a legacy that would last long after he went to his heavenly reward. In his younger years, just making it through another day was enough, but now, he recognized that putting some thought to tomorrow was more desirable.

Heck figured the best way to find Vega was to start at one end of the street and work his way through each and every saloon, gambling hall, and bordello, until he found his man. If he struck out in the more reputable establishments, he would be forced to search the flop houses and opium tents on the lower side of town.

Elbowing his way past a couple of drunk vaqueros, Heck made his way through the first cantina. He hoped he would see Luis before the killer saw him first, but between the games of chance and the spinning skirts of the young ladies, Heck saw that no one was paying any attention to him at all. After ordering a beer, he found a place at the bar where he could look over the faces of the patrons without rousing any suspicion. The cantina's customers were a rough lot, and Heck was sure there was probably more than one killer and horse thief in the bunch, but the one he was looking for was not among them.

For an hour, Heck moved from one smoke filled saloon to another, staying long enough in each to have a beer and a quick look around. As he was beginning to think he was in for a long night, he finally caught a glimpse of a familiar face. Seated at a back table, Luis Vega was engaged in lively conversation with two other men and a woman, who was obviously less interested in the men's conversation than she was in the drinks they were buying her.

Walking up next to Vega, Heck pressed the barrel of his Peacemaker into the man's ribs and pulled back the hammer. "Hello, Luis. That's a .45 you feel pressed against your side, so unless ya wanna be carried outta here, you'd best stand up and walk towards the door with me."

Pulling Vega's pistol from his holster, Heck motioned for the other two men to drop their guns as well.

Turning to the woman, Heck gave her a smile and said, "Señorita, por favor."

After the woman left to find someone else to buy her drinks, he grabbed Vega by the arm and pulled him to his feet.

"You are a very determined man, Señor," Luis said good-naturedly. "You come all this way just for one man?"

Shoving the man towards the door, Heck said, "Well, you're a mighty important man back in Texas, Luis. There's a man back there with a rope who's expecting you."

"You've got to get me there first, señor, and like you said, I've got nothing to lose."

Grabbing Luis by the hair, he pulled his face to within inches of his own. "Listen to me very carefully, if you give me a minute's trouble on the way back, I'll shoot you in both knees and take you back to Texas tied across your saddle."

"I see your point, señor, but I think maybe it's you who needs the date with a rope more than me. At least I'm honest about what I do. I'm not hiding my bad deeds behind a badge or some piece of paper written by the governor."

"You might be right, Luis, but sometimes life just don't work out like it should. Now, get moving."

As they were about to reach the door, three men stepped in front of them and blocked their path.

"We're not letting you leave with our friend, gringo," one of the men said.

"Stand aside," Heck said. "I'm a lawman from Texas, and Mister Vega is my prisoner."

"He's a bounty hunter, and he's got no power here," Luis said. "If you kill him, I'll make you all rich men."

Heck tightened his grip on Vega and pushed the barrel of his gun into the outlaw's back. "I'm gonna give you boys one more chance to get outta my way and then I'm gonna start shooting. You'll probably kill me, but your friend will die in the process, and you'll never see the riches he promised you."

"You make me laugh, gringo. You think you can come into our town and take our friend. Money means nothing to us, and we'll be happy to kill you for free."

The formerly chaotic saloon slowly turned silent, as the customers eagerly awaited the shooting fight they were sure would follow. Nobody was giving the Texan much chance of making it through the door alive, but he seemed so confident and they couldn't wait to see what he had up his sleeve.

Heck himself wasn't quite sure what he would do next, and he hoped that his outward display of bravado would carry him through until he thought of something. The men knew that Luis Vega would likely be killed by either Heck or in the crossfire, so they had not yet made a play for their guns, but Heck knew from experience that once the threats were made, violence was inevitable.

As Heck stared at the men, he saw their eyes narrowing and prepared himself for the fight that was about to explode.

The three men instinctively took several steps away from each other, making it less likely that Heck would be able to kill all three. Their hands slowly inched closer to their guns, but before they could make their play, the sound of a lever-action rifle being cocked broke the silence.

"Keep your hands away from those guns, boys," a voice from the street called out. "I've got a Winchester pointed at your backs."

Forgotten Country John Spiars

The voice sounded vaguely familiar to Heck, though he couldn't quite remember where he had heard it. As he took a deep breath at the sudden and unexpected interference on his behalf, he tried to place the voice of his benefactor.

The three men raised their arms perpendicular to the ground as the sound of the stranger's boots echoed on the wooden boardwalk, his spurs chiming with each step.

"That's real good," the stranger said, as he walked through the doorway. "Just stay where you are and me and my friend will leave you in peace."

Looking into the face of the man who had come to his aid, Heck recognized his old friend at once.

"Paul? Paul Broward?" Heck exclaimed.

"Yes, it's me, Heck, but maybe we should save the pleasantries until we've hoofed it outta town."

"Well, I reckon now would be as good a time as any to leave, but this man's my prisoner, and he's coming with us."

Holding his rifle on the others, Paul nodded his head and said, "You fellas heard my friend. All three of us are leaving, and anybody that sticks their head out that door will be getting a bullet for their trouble. C'mon, Heck, let's get outta here."

Chapter Five

From the top of a distant hill, Heck peered through his spy glass, checking their back trail.

"I don't see anybody following us. I reckon them boys were more interested in staying in their nice, safe saloon than tangling with the likes of us."

"Good," Paul said, "cause I ain't real interested in tangling with them either."

"I'm glad you came along when ya did," Heck said, shaking the man's hand, "but what were ya doing there?"

"I was in town on ranch business and saw you going from saloon to saloon. I heard you'd taken up bounty hunting, so I figured you must be searching for somebody and thought ya might need someone watching your backside. Turns out, I was right."

Heck couldn't put his finger on it, maybe it was Paul showing up right when he needed him, or maybe it was the hesitation in his voice, but Heck knew he wasn't telling him the truth. As a lawman, Heck was used to people being dishonest, and he had learned to sniff out even the best lies. He couldn't figure why a man he considered a friend wouldn't be straight with him, but he consoled himself that at least Paul wasn't so used to lying that he'd become good at it.

"How'd ya know I was a bounty hunter?" Heck asked, climbing into the saddle.

"Dang, Heck," Paul replied. "Don't ya know? You're famous, at least in this part of the country. It's been all over the newspapers, how you've been working with the governor to clean up Texas. I'm glad to see you went back to being a lawman after Colorado. How about Jim and Red? Did they go back to Texas, too?"

"No, the last I heard, Red was busy making another fortune in Leadville, and Jim was still a town marshal, but I ain't heard news of 'em in several years. What about you? Are you still working for Mister Kraft?"

"Yeah, I reckon I'll be riding for his brand as long as he's got two cows that need tending," Paul said.

"The cow business is still treating him good, then?" Heck asked, looking over his shoulder to be sure his prisoner was still bringing up the rear.

"As long as people have a taste for beef, we'll still be selling it to 'em, but it ain't all been milk and honey."

"What do ya mean?"

"After Bartlow's men raided the ranch and so many of our men were killed, Mister Kraft changed," Paul said hesitantly, not sure if he should be telling any of this to Heck. After a moment, he decided that since the words had already been said, he might as well continue. "He made a vow to never be led like a lamb to slaughter again. We brought on more men, many of 'em soldiers from the war, and all with orders to kill at the least trouble. I can't even tell ya how many cattle thieves we've hung in the last year."

"Bartlow's men were a bad bunch for sure," Heck said, "but we caught up to 'em and sure enough made 'em pay for what they done. I had hoped that would have been enough to give Mister Kraft some peace at the loss of his men."

"I don't think he has much interest in peace," Paul said. "He'll be glad to see you, though. He feels he owes you, Jim and Red a debt for helping us. If y'all hadn't been there, those men might have killed us all."

"He don't owe us anything, but I'm looking forward to seeing him again, too. I appreciate the offer to put up at the ranch for a few days. I've been on the trail after Vega for weeks, and I could use a few days of rest and good meals before heading back to Texas."

"The rest I can provide, but I don't know about good food. We still have the same cook, and his victuals ain't improved any over the years. You never told me why you were tracking this fellow. What did he do?"

"Him and his brother are wanted for murder and horse theft. Me and one of my ranch hands captured his brother, Benito, in El Paso, but Luis got away."

"He sounds like a bad man," Paul said, his voice trailing off a bit as he stared into the night sky. "I'm glad I was able to do my part to bring this one to justice. He deserves what he's got coming."

As he listened to Paul, Heck was once again getting the sense the man wasn't playing him straight, and he was beginning to think he would be better off to forget about resting up, and just head back to Texas immediately.

The men rode through the rest of the night and most of the next day in almost total silence. By the time they began to descend the small mountain range that lay just to the west of the Kraft Ranch, Heck was getting the feeling that Paul wished he had just gone back to Texas as well. The closer the men got to their destination, the more nervous Paul seemed to become, and Heck was certain he was in for more than a happy reunion with old friends.

Paul Broward and his boss, Victor Kraft, had gone out of their way to save Heck, Jim and Red when they were in a bad way. Heck considered both men to be good friends, so the dread that seemed to be building with each mile they rode could not be explained, but Heck had learned to trust his gut and right now, it told him he was riding into trouble.

Once the three men had descended the little mountain, the green pasture land of the Kraft Ranch stretched out before them, a turbulent sea of green, pitching and rolling in the soft breeze.

Looking from the puffs of foamy clouds moving along the azure background, to the endless stretch of prairie grass, Heck breathed in the peaceful world that appeared far removed from the violence that had made up most of his life. Gazing out over the beautiful vista, it occurred to him that what he was seeing was nothing more than an illusion that was hiding something deadly lurking in the shadows. He had heard of outlaws who used pretty girls to lure in unsuspecting cowboys, so they could be robbed, and he recognized that what he was seeing now wasn't much different.

"It's beautiful, ain't it," Paul said, interrupting Heck's thoughts, "but it's deceiving and comes at a dear price."

"What do you mean, Paul?" Heck asked, reining his appaloosa to a stop. "It seems you've spent the last hundred miles trying to tell me something, so stop beating around the bush and just spit it out."

Without speaking, Paul continued to ride, as though he didn't hear what Heck had said. When he was a good ten feet ahead of him, he turned around in the saddle. "I don't know what ya mean, Heck, I was just making conversation. We're only a few miles from the house, and it would probably be best if I rode ahead and talked to Mister Kraft. I'm sure the boss will be happy to have you, but I'd best let him know that you're bringing a prisoner with ya. He's a bit touchy about such things these days."

"Whatever ya think is best, Paul," Heck said, gently nudging his horse with his spurs.

Heck continued leading his prisoner down the worn cattle path and watched as Paul's horse loped out of sight.

"We need to get out of here," Luis Vega said in an urgent tone that was almost pleading. "If we get to that house, we are both dead."

"What are you talking about?" Heck demanded. "The man who owns this ranch is an old friend of mine. What did you do to him that you fear him so much?"

"I might have relieved them of a few miserable horses, but nothing to deserve what they have planned for me."

"What difference does it make to you where you die? You've got a date with the hangman once I get you back to Texas anyway."

"There are many ways to die, señor. Your friends Paul and Kraft are quite gifted at finding the most painful ways to kill their enemies."

"You're a liar, Luis," Heck said. While he realized that time may have indeed hardened the men he had known, he refused to believe they had gone down such a bad path. "We are going to the ranch for supplies and so I can rest, but you're my prisoner and you'll be leaving with me when I start back to Texas."

"You're a fool," Luis said, grabbing the lead rope and pulling it from Heck's hands.

With the skill of a master horseman, Luis turned his horse and spurred it back towards the mountain range. Before Heck realized what had happened, Vega had his horse at a dead run, and was almost a quarter of a mile ahead.

Cussing himself for letting a prisoner get the best of him, Heck put spur to horse, and set out to retrieve Vega. The man might have been an outlaw, but he could handle a horse better than anyone Heck had seen in a long time. He could tell he'd have to have a little luck on his side if he hoped to stop Luis before he reached sanctuary among the hazardous mountain trails.

His appaloosa lunged with its front legs at each step, as the scenery flashed by in a blur. The trail ascending to the top of the range loomed less than a mile in the distance, and Heck feared that if Luis made it there, he would become lost among the labyrinth of trails and caverns.

With less than a quarter mile before Vega reached probable freedom, Heck received the bit of luck he had hoped for. A group of wild pigs crossed the trail in front of Vega, causing his horse to pull up short. Luis dug his boot heels into the stirrups to avoid being thrown over the animal's neck, but as his horse came to a stop, it turned, dumping Vega sideways off its back.

After determining that he hadn't sustained any permanent injury, Luis painfully pulled himself to his feet, as Heck stood over him with Colt in hand.

"That was some mighty fine riding, Luis. If those pigs hadn't got in your way, you might have made it. Now, get back on your horse, and if you try that again, I'll shoot you in the back and call it a day."

"Ya can't blame a man for trying to save his own neck, señor. Trust me, the time will come very soon when you will be sorry you didn't just let me escape."

Chapter Six

Even though it had been more than ten years since Heck had set foot on the Kraft Ranch, he was able to locate the road leading to the ranch houses without any problem.

As the two men rode through the main yard and up to the bunk house, they passed a line of Kraft's men, standing at attention like a professional army. They were all hard men, nothing like the good-natured cowboys that had been devoted to Kraft. While they would undoubtedly kill for their boss, they would never have the same sense of loyalty to a brand that they had for money.

"Howdy, Heck," Paul called out. "I'm glad to see ya remembered how to find the place."

"I wasn't sure myself, but it all came back to me," Heck said, helping Luis Vega down from his horse.

"We're not very well set up for holding prisoners," Paul said, "but I reckon the ice house should hold him. I'll have a couple of the hands take him there."

"That's alright," Heck replied. "I can take him there myself."

"Suit yourself," Paul said. "I'll show you the way, and then we'll go see Mister Kraft."

As the men escorted Luis Vega down the narrow path that led behind the main house, Heck's questions could no longer go unanswered.

"Kraft sure does have a lot of boys working for him these days."

"Like I told you, business has been good, and we had to take on more hands."

"Most of them boys are gun hands, not cow hands. It looks like y'all are preparing for a war instead of a cattle drive."

"I don't know what you mean, Heck," Paul said. "They're just a bunch of cowboys."

"Don't lie to me, Paul," Heck said. "I can recognize professional gunfighters when I see 'em. What's going on here?"

"You can walk your prisoner in," Paul said, opening the door to the icehouse.

With a lantern in hand, Heck led Luis Vega down the stone steps of the icehouse. "If you want to be fed regular, I suggest you behave yourself while we're here."

"I'll do whatever you say, but please don't let them kill me. This place is muy malo, very bad," Vega said, grabbing Heck by the arm.

"Nobody will be killing you, except the duly appointed officers of the court back in Texas. Now, sit down and do what you're told."

Walking back up the stairs, Heck couldn't shake the terror that had stricken Luis Vega since they had arrived at the ranch. There was an air of menace that filled every corner of the ranch, and even Paul was unrecognizable as the man he had once known.

"Do you reckon it'll hold him?" Paul asked, as Heck exited the building.

"It should do," Heck said, "but I don't reckon he'll be any trouble. He's been here before, hasn't he Paul?"

"Why would you say that? That don't make no sense at all."

"Luis Vega is a hardened killer, and yet he's terrified of you. That's what don't make no sense. Tell me what's going on."

"Those are questions best left for later, Mister Carson," a voice called from the shadows.

Straining through the twilight darkness to find the identity of the speaker, Heck instantly recognized Victor Kraft as he stepped into the lamp light.

"Mister Kraft, it's good to see you again."

"Thank you, Heck. It's good to see you as well. Please follow me to my house. Supper is on the table, and from what Paul has told me, you could use a good meal."

"He's right about that, but I need the truth even more."

"All your questions will be answered, but in the house, not out here in the open."

As he followed Kraft, Heck was surprised to find the rancher he had remembered, and not the vicious animal he had come to expect.

In the ornate formal dining room, supper was served on a long, wooden table, which was intricately carved, with high-back chairs to match. The spread was as elaborate as the table itself and consisted of roasted pork, potatoes, greens, and a heavy bread loaf.

While Heck was more interested in hearing what Victor Kraft had to say than eating, the precarious life of a frontier lawman had taught him to take food when it was available. He ate two full plates and drank a pitcher of cold well water before prodding Kraft to finally answer his questions.

"Thank you for supper, Mister Kraft, but I really must know what is going on around here."

"What do you mean?" Kraft said slyly. "The only thing that's going on is a couple of old friends having a nice meal together."

"I'm talking about the army of gunfighters you've taken on. Even Paul here is wearing his pistol tied down."

"You think I'm a gun tough, Heck?" Paul said, jumping to his feet. "Sure, I've learned how to use a gun since we last saw each other, but I'm still just a cowboy."

Victor Kraft stood up at the end of the table and poured three drinks from a glass decanter. "Heck, the last time we saw each other, I had just buried some mighty fine men. They were killed by wolves who saw this ranch as easy pickings, who saw us as lambs to be slaughtered. If it wasn't for you and your friends, our losses would have been even greater. If you'll recall, I asked ya to stay, but you had vengeance on your mind, so other arrangements had to be made. You think my men are a group of cutthroats, but I would wager that not any two of them have sent as many to their graves as you."

Heck took a long sip of the whiskey that Kraft had set before him, chewing over all that Victor Kraft had told him.

"Perhaps that is true, but my killin' has been in service of the law and during war time, not to put money in my pocket. I've been told that a rustler would have better odds with the pox than being found on Kraft land."

Kraft downed his whiskey and slammed his fist on the table. "I will not be judged by you. New Mexico Territory is not Texas. We are still an unsettled land, where a man has to be willing to fight to keep what is his. Those that choose to support themselves on the hard work of others will come to a quick end around here, and I will not apologize for that. You are a welcomed guest on my ranch, and I hope you will accept my hospitality for as long as you need to rest up. I have prepared a room for you here in the main house, but I assume you will want to look in on your prisoner before turning in. I will have Xavier fix him a plate of food and a pitcher of water. That is the extent of the kindness I intend to show to that killer and thief."

After Victor Kraft excused himself, Paul stood beside Heck, and in a hushed tone said, "Mister Kraft respects you, Heck, and he was very happy at the thought of seeing you again. I hope you're not going to take the word of an outlaw over that of old friends. I'll take you back to the icehouse, so you can check on your prisoner, and then I'll show you to your room."

Heck stretched on the large bed after seeing that his prisoner was fed. The bed was the softest he had enjoyed in some time, and he wouldn't have minded a few more nights of such comfort, but despite Victor Kraft's offer, Heck couldn't help but feel he would be pushing his luck if he stayed. After a good night's sleep, he figured to get his prisoner and hit the trail. With any luck, he would be miles down the road before anyone on the ranch knew he was gone.

Chapter Seven

A distinct cry of terror echoed through the walls of the cavernous house, causing Heck to jerk awake, pistol in hand. It was a hollow sound, as though it rose from the bottom of a deep well, and after the veil of sleep had faded from his brain, he wondered if he had really heard it at all.

As his bare feet stepped onto the cold wood floor, he strained to hear the sound again, but he was greeted only by deafening silence.

Heck quickly pulled his boots on, grabbed his pistol belt, and donned his frock coat. He ran down the hallway and bounded down the stairs two at a time, expecting Mister Kraft to appear at any moment, investigating the source of all the commotion. Heading out the front door, the thought occurred to him that he had been the only one in the house, which naturally begged the question, "Where was everyone else?"

Approaching the icehouse, the first thing that caught Heck's eye was that the door was cracked open. Rushing into the stone structure, he drew his Colt and carefully made his way down the steps, but aside from a few blocks of ice, the room was empty.

Heck ran from the icehouse to the kitchen and then to the horse barn, but there was not so much as one man to be found.

Reaching into his saddlebag, he pulled out his spyglass and began scanning the pastures surrounding the ranch, but other than a few hundred head of cattle, there was nothing to be seen. He aimed his glass to the north, east, then to the south, and just when he thought that the earth had opened and swallowed up everyone but him, Heck saw several points of light in the distance. The source of the light was at least a mile to the south, so he saddled up his horse and Vega's as well, not sure what he was going to find.

The sky was covered by thick clouds and the only illumination during his ride south were the flashes of lightning that streaked across the western horizon.

Stopping occasionally to peer through his spyglass, Heck saw that the points of light were actually torches arranged in a circle, only a few hundred yards in front of him. He nudged his appaloosa forward at a slow walk, trying to conjure some reasonable explanation for what was going on, but nothing came to mind. Whatever it was he was riding into, Heck knew it couldn't be anything good.

At the edge of a small clearing, Heck tied both horses and crept the rest of the way on foot. He measured each step, careful not to step on anything that would give himself away, though the sound of many voices, all speaking at once, was growing louder, and would have drowned out all but the loudest noise.

From the cover of the trees, Heck looked out on a scene that he wouldn't have believed had he not looked on it with his own eyes. The men of the Kraft Ranch stood in a circle, each carrying a torch, surrounding a large pyre made of felled trees. Tied to the pyramid of wood was Luis Vega, screaming for mercy at the top of his lungs, but judging by the anger in the voices of the assembled crowd, his pleas were falling on deaf ears.

For a brief moment, Heck considered getting back on his horse and riding for Texas, leaving Vega to the fate he probably deserved. After all, what would be gained by sticking his neck out for the outlaw? He would more than likely earn a horrible death along with Vega, or he would be forced to shoot it out with friends who had once saved his life. Even if he did manage to escape with his prisoner, he would only be taking Luis Vega back to Texas to face another date with death. In the end, Heck knew he had no choice, he represented the law, and Luis Vega would answer to a jury for his crimes, not a group of vigilantes.

Night was beginning to give way to the first light of morning, and Heck realized that Vega's time was running out. If he was going to make his move, it would have to be now.

Wiping his brow on his sleeve, Heck drew a deep breath and stepped into the clearing. The assembled crowd was worked up into such a blood-fueled frenzy, they wouldn't have noticed him if he'd been covered in feathers and clucked like a chicken.

Forgotten Country   John Spiars

Walking from the shade of the trees and into the rays of sun that were beginning to stream into the clearing, Heck made his presence known.

"What's going on here?" he yelled.

As the men turned to see who was speaking, a hush settled over the mob, broke only by the call of a nightingale somewhere in the distance.

"Mister Carson, what are you doing here?" Victor Kraft said, pushing his way through the throng of men.

"That's my question to you," Heck said.

"Heck, you need to get out of here," Paul said, as he held his gun on Vega. "Get back to the house, and we'll be along directly."

"No, it's alright, Heck. You should stay and see this," Victor said.

"See what?" Heck said.

"An example of what happens to murdering horse thieves who think they can steal from me and get away with it."

"Help me!" Vega cried out. "They're gonna burn me alive! You've got to stop them."

"Shut up," Paul snapped, "or I'll shoot ya myself."

"Mister Kraft, you can't do this," Heck pleaded. "You're a good man, not a savage."

Several of Kraft's gunhands began to move toward Heck, but their boss signaled them to hold their ground.

"Mister Carson. Heck. This isn't a fight you want, not for this scum. Paul tells me you're starting a ranch of your own. Well, you'll see for yourself that if you're going to hold onto what you've got, you must strike fear into the hearts of the rabble that would take what is yours."

"Heck, you don't know what it was like before," Paul said, stepping forward so he could be heard. "After the war we had every outlaw and cutthroat in the territory nipping at our heels. We were on the verge of going bust like many other ranches around here, but we finally said 'enough' and drew a line in the sand. We've shown the outlaws that we can be just as barbaric as they are, and they're finally getting the message. Until Mister Vega came along, we hadn't been hit in almost a year."

"Wrong is wrong," Heck said, "and your reasons don't change that. You must have known that I wouldn't just let you take my prisoner, that's why you lied to me about your intentions."

"You were never supposed to be here," Paul said. "We heard Vega was in Santa Fe and I was sent to capture him and bring him back. It was just bad luck you found him first. I didn't want to lie to you. We figured we could do what had to be done, and you'd go back to Texas."

"Well, what's the plan now?" Heck said, walking past Kraft, and making his way to Vega.

"The plan hasn't changed," Kraft said. "We're going to send this man to hell, and you'll go back to Texas empty-handed."

"That ain't happening. He's my prisoner and he's leaving with me. You'd better tell your men to stand aside or Luis Vega won't be the only one making the trip to hades."

"That's your choice I suppose, but just remember, this isn't what I wanted," Kraft said. "Alright, boys, light him up."

A scrawny wisp of a man, wearing double pistols in a cross-draw holster, stepped forward, carrying a pail of kerosene. He reared back and began dousing Luis with the flammable liquid, sloshing it on several others who were standing close by.

"Mister Kraft, tell your man to stop before things happen that can't be taken back," Heck said, pulling his Colt Lightning from his back.

"Can we go ahead and burn this horse thief or are we gonna take orders from this Texan trash," the scrawny gunslinger said, grabbing a torch from one of his friends.

"Take another step with that torch and I'll shoot ya where ya stand," Heck said.

"Get to it," Kraft called out, "and if Mister Carson interferes, you are to shoot him dead."

"Yes sir," the man said, moving toward Luis Vega.

"Wait," Paul said. "We're not shooting Heck, and maybe we should forget about killing Vega too."

"You forget yourself, sir," Kraft said. "I give the orders on this ranch, and I say the thief shall burn. Anyone that tries to stop it is to be killed on the spot."

"But sir—" Paul started, before he was interrupted by Kraft.

"Silence, Mister Broward, before I have you dragged off my property. Now, I demand you men do what we come here for."

"You heard the boss," the gunslinger said, "if anybody tries to stop me, fill 'em full of lead." Bringing his arm back, the man prepared to toss his torch at Vega, but a bullet from Heck's Colt ended his effort, and his life.

Falling backwards, the dead gunman flung the torch from his hand, which ignited two of the gun hands who had been doused by kerosene. As the men screamed in pain, their flaming bodies set off a wall of fire across the kerosene-soaked ground and created a hellish panic that would have made Dante proud.

Seizing his opportunity, Heck shoved Victor Kraft to the ground and made his way to Vega, cutting the ropes that bound the outlaw. Heck tried to make his escape, but before he could take a step, Paul was in front of him with pistol in hand.

Heck put his hands up and tried to appeal to his former friend, but Paul pulled the trigger twice without waiting to hear what Heck had to say.

For a moment, Heck really thought he was dead until he looked behind him and saw two more of Kraft's gunfighters fall to the ground.

"Take your prisoner and get out of here," Paul said, firing into the flames at the remaining gunhands, who were beginning to regain their senses and starting to mount an offensive.

"I'm not gonna leave you to face this by yourself," Heck said, drawing his other gun.

Between the two men, they managed to take down three more of the hired killers, but neither man had enough ammunition to win a fight against the six remaining gunmen.

The flames spread across the clearing, fueled by the dry grass and brisk morning breeze. Within a few moments, the conflagration would spread to the trees, cutting off any hope of escape.

"Get out of here, now," Paul hollered, above the ravenous chaos exploding around them.

As the gunmen began to press forward, Heck emptied his pistols into their midst, after which, he grabbed Vega by the arm and pulled him across the burning field.

"You'd better come with us, Paul," Heck said. "I think your prospects here have come to an end."

Making it to the trees, the three men were only seconds ahead of their pursuing enemy, who were firing wildly as they ran.

"They ain't much good at shooting on the run," Heck said, "but our good luck and their bad aim will likely end before long."

"It was good seeing you again, Heck. Get your prisoner back to Texas."

Dropping to one knee, Paul turned and fired the two shots he had left, knocking one of the men to the ground.

"Paul, get up and come with us. You'll die if you stay here."

"Get going," Paul replied. "I can buy ya a few seconds at most."

Not wanting to leave his friend, but also not wanting his sacrifice to be in vain, Heck continued pulling Luis through the trees to where he left their horses.

Jumping to his feet, Paul charged at the approaching men, wielding his empty pistol like a club. He took two shots to the chest, but still managed to deliver a vicious blow to the man at the head of the mob. Another shot caught Paul Broward in the left temple, causing him to fall backwards, a look of calm permanently etched on his face.

As Heck and Vega were finally within sight of the horses, several bullets struck the trees only inches from their heads.

"You made a fine effort, but it looks like we're gonna die on this cursed ranch, after all," Vega said, ducking his head as gunshots whizzed by their ears.

"We ain't dying here," Heck said, pushing the man into a brushy thicket.

With the last bit of stamina he could muster, Heck pushed for the horses, with two gunmen only steps behind him.

Reaching his horse, Heck leapt into the air and managed to get his boot into the stirrup. He lifted himself into the air over the horse's back. As he sailed over the appaloosa's body, he reached down and pulled his shotgun from its boot. Landing hard on his back, he shook off the pain and pulled the hammer back on both barrels. From the cold grass, Heck took aim at the two men and let loose with both loads, opening up an enormous hole in the unlucky gunmen.

"Vega, get over here," he called, untying both horses and turning them back up the trail. "We gotta ride hard."

With the flames and grey smoke rising above the trees, and the angry shouts of the few men still living echoing in the distance, Heck and Vega urged their horses up the trail as fast as they could manage and made their way off the Kraft Ranch. The Texas border was several hundred miles away, but neither man planned on slowing down until they were safely back in the Lone Star State.

CHAPTER EIGHT

For over a week, Heck pushed himself and Luis Vega through the mountains and across the desert of southern New Mexico. The trek over the mountains was the most arduous part of the journey, as Heck had to both keep watch over his prisoner and his back trail, against the possibility that Kraft's killers might be in pursuit.

Surviving on almost no sleep, Heck would travel until sunset, and then after feeding and securing his prisoner, he would retrace their trail to scout for any pursuers. Each night, upon returning to camp, he would have only a few hours before sun up in which to sleep.

Once they came out of the high country and into the desert, Heck reversed the process, and began traveling by night and sleeping during the day. The flat land allowed Heck to watch their back trail for many miles, enabling him to get more sleep instead of having to back track for hours each night. There was a drastic downside to their new circumstances, however. They no longer had the easy access to fresh water and game that they had in the mountains and were forced to make due with just a few sips of water and a bit of wild turnips each day.

After eating their meager repast, the two men would settle under the shade of a large rock to sleep. Heck slept in short, restless spurts, with his Greener shotgun resting across his leg. The sweltering heat made it almost impossible to fall asleep and slumber was achieved only after extreme exhaustion took control over their senses.

Crossing the border into El Paso, Heck and Luis were nearly starved and had to catch their sleep from the saddle, because neither had the strength to climb on and off their horses.

"Well, my friend," Vega said, with a broad smile, "it appears we have once again reached civilization. I will take you to a place with the best food you've ever tasted, and afterwards, the tequila will flow like mother's milk."

"You must have spent too much time out in that sun," Heck said, urging both horses down the trail. "I'm not following you into town where your friends can bushwhack me again. I'll find someone along the way and pay them to bring us back some food and water. I might have saved you from being burned alive, but I'm still turning you over to the sheriff in Fort Stockton. You're a killer and thief, and you have a date with the hangman."

"My friend, you are stubbornly attached to this law of yours. It makes no sense," Vega said with an exasperated sigh.

"I'm sure it doesn't," Heck said with a slight smile, "and stop calling me friend."

Forgotten Country — John Spiars

If Heck had not been so physically exhausted from lack of sleep, food and water, it might have occurred to him that Vega was being especially cocky for a man on his way to the gallows. As it was, though, he just put it off as the mental deficiency of a vicious killer who couldn't come to square with his impending death.

At a crossroads a few miles outside of El Paso, Heck flagged down a teenage boy. The young man was leading a burro which pulled a small wooden cart, loaded down with vegetables and various other sundries to sell in town.

"Hola, amigo," Heck said warmly.

"Hello, señor," the boy replied, as he eyed the two men warily, understandably suspicious of being stopped by strangers on a deserted road. Highwaymen were still common along the lonely rural roads of west Texas, and many a traveler met an untimely end at their hands.

"Ah, you speak English," Heck said with a smile. "That's good, cause my Spanish ain't much better than passable. My friend and I were hoping you might help a couple of weary travelers by bringing us back some food and water."

"Maybe you men have time to stop and help strangers," the young man said, as he continued to tug at the mule's harness, "but my family is depending on me to sell everything in this wagon. We need the money to buy more seed and maybe a hog or two."

Heck admired the boy's pluck and his devotion to his family and he could see the young man would drive a shrewd bargain.

"What if we bought some of your vegetables just to eat on until you come back with something heartier. I will, of course, pay you for your trouble as well."

The boy stopped the wagon, obviously interested in Heck's offer, but still not ready to trust him completely.

"Why can't you just go into town and get your own food?"

"Let's just say, we'd rather some people didn't know we were around, but that's our business. Your business is feeding your family, which at the moment, means feeding us."

"I will do it, Señor."

Heck gave the boy some money and lifted a basket of fresh greens out of the wagon.

"I will return soon with such a feast as has never been seen," he said, excitedly counting the money Heck had handed him.

"Thank you," Heck said.

"Yes, thank you," Luis Vega said, reaching out and shaking the young man's hand.

As the boy slowly urged the ornery burro forward, Heck and Vega quickly began devouring the basket of greens which also contained a few large carrots.

The two men set up a make shift camp under a stand of trees just off the main road. From there, Heck could watch the trail without being easily seen. Leaning against a tree, enjoying the cool shade of its branches, Heck let out a sigh as the weight of his own fatigue pressed down on him. He hoped the boy wouldn't dawdle long in town as he knew he must get his prisoner to Fort Stockton before his body gave in to its desire for rest. The thought that the boy would not return never entered Heck's mind, realizing the young man would not pass on the opportunity to help his family.

Forgotten Country								John Spiars

In little more than an hour, any fear Heck may have had was put to rest as he saw the figure of the young man running up the trail. He carried a tote sack that, judging by the way the boy struggled under its weight, must have been full of provisions.

The boy stood at the crossroads, looking for the two men. Heck reluctantly pulled himself up and waved his arms until the kid saw their hiding place.

"You made it back in good time," Heck said, closing his pocket watch and placing it back in his vest pocket. "You will be well rewarded for your troubles."

"Thank you, señor, but I'm afraid others were willing to pay more. Please don't think it's just about the money. Me and my family must do business in El Paso."

Before Heck was able to catch the meaning of the young man's words, three men with rifles appeared out of the trees.

"Please don't move, señor," the man in front said. "The death you have earned will not be fulfilled by the gun."

"Who are you?" Heck asked, shading his eyes with his hand so he could get a better look at the man speaking.

"My name is Tomas. You killed Fernando, our Jefe, and we have been hoping to meet you again, but we didn't think it would be so soon."

"Perhaps instead of searching me for weapons, you should have taken my pencil," Luis Vega said, laughing. "I slipped the boy a note, offering a great reward if he brought back help. It would seem what they say is true, the pen is stronger than the sword. I am sorry it had to come to this, but like you said, we are not friends."

"Why are you laughing, estupido?" Tomas said, turning his rifle on Vega. "It was you and your fool of a brother that brought this man here, so you are also the cause of Fernando dying."

The first shot knocked Luis off his feet, and would probably have finished him, but the outlaws put four more bullets in him just for good measure, and as vengeance for their dead boss.

Leaning over, Heck seized the opportunity to make his move and pulled his shotgun from its scabbard. Raising and cocking it in one fluid motion, Heck caught two of the men standing together and pulled the trigger of both barrels.

Heck fell to the ground ahead of a volley of shots from Tomas' rifle and drew his pistol. Fanning the hammer as quickly as he could, he managed to put three shots into the man's chest. All three rounds struck Tomas in a group no larger than a silver dollar, and suddenly all the practice Heck had put in with the Peacemaker didn't seem like such a waste of time.

Spinning around, Heck aimed his pistol at the young man who had betrayed him.

"I am sorry, señor. Please don't kill me. I know I deserve to die, but my mother and sisters will not survive without me," the boy pleaded.

"I'm not gonna kill ya, kid," Heck said, putting his pistol back in its holster. "You did what you had to do to keep your family safe. Help me bury these fellas and you can keep anything they have of value, but I would stay out of El Paso for a while. The law will be looking for them for a time, but they will soon tire of searching."

"Thank you, señor."

"You can call me Heck. We have much work ahead of us, and we'll be good friends by the time we're done."

"I'm sorry about the other man too. His death is my fault."

"He was not a good man, and he was gonna die one way or another. I reckon here under these trees is as good a place for him to meet his end as any other. We'd better get to our work."

Chapter Nine

The town of Uvalde was enjoying an infrequent cool spell, where the breeze came from just the right direction to flow down Main Street, drawing most of the town from the stifling heat of their shops and homes.

As Heck rode through the center of town, the citizens eyed the haggard, dirty figure suspiciously, as they did all strangers since the O'Shea gang had terrorized the town only a few years previous. In his present condition, Heck was unrecognizable to the townspeople as the hero who had rid them of the O'Shea's.

Heck reined his horse to a stop in front of the hotel, but instead of the warm homecoming he expected, his hackles were raised by the familiar sense of impending trouble.

Forgotten Country — John Spiars

He climbed down from his horse, more than a little confused by the behavior of the people he considered friends. Two men he recognized were seated just outside the door of the hotel, but as they stared at Heck, the two offered no greeting at all.

"Howdy, Ernesto. Howdy, Doc White," he said, addressing the hotel owner and doctor.

Both men rose to their feet, staring at Heck as though he were some savage looking to cut their throats.

"Howdy, friend," Doc said. "Do we know you?"

"Dang it, Doc. It's me, Heck."

"Heck? My goodness, son. What happened to you?" Doc said, grabbing his hand and shaking it vigorously. "I've pulled the shroud over men who looked better than you."

"Señor Heck, is that really you?" Ernesto said.

"Yep, it's me. I reckon I do look a might rough, but I've spent the last month on the trail of an outlaw, and I ain't had much of a chance to keep myself proper. I ain't been within spitting distance of enough water to drink, much less to bathe in."

"Look everybody, Heck's come back to us," Doc White yelled to everyone within the sound of his voice.

As a huge crowd of welcoming faces gathered around him and slapped his back, Heck looked past them, searching the street for the one person he really cared about seeing. After a few moments, he saw a beautiful woman with dark features, rushing to the opposite side of the street and then out of view, and he knew it was Caroline Farber.

He dismissed those gathered around him as politely as he knew how, and then quickly slipped into the hotel, followed by Ernesto.

"Do you want your usual room, señor?" Ernesto asked, stepping behind the desk.

"Yes, please, and a hot tub. Can you have my horse taken to the livery for feed and a brush down? Tell 'em I'll be by directly to settle the payment."

After a bath and knocking as much of the dirt off his clothes as possible, Heck made his way downstairs to the lobby.

"Your horse has been taken care of, señor," Ernesto said.

"Thank you, my friend. Does Miss Farber still take evening meals at the café?"

"I believe she does. Her and Mister Snow are usually there around this time."

"Is that so?" Heck said, suddenly angry, though he didn't quite understand why. "Who is Mister Snow?"

"He is a banker and owns most of the businesses in town," Ernesto said. "He came to town soon after you left and began spreading his money around. He's been courting Miss Farber for many months," he added with obvious embarrassment.

Walking into the café, Heck looked around, and then as usual, chose a table in the back with a good view of the door. As Heck made his way to the back, he passed Caroline Farber's table. She was sitting with a tall, lean man who had the look of someone who commanded much respect, but he also seemed strangely out of place in Uvalde. His suit was made of wool and perfectly tailored, but not the sort of thing men in Uvalde wore. The mustache that covered his upper lip was waxed to a point at both ends and his goatee was trimmed so that it formed a triangle just above his chin. Heck couldn't help but think he looked similar to all the drawings he had ever seen of the devil, and he figured that appearance wasn't the only thing he shared in common with Old Scratch.

Tipping his hat to the lady, he moved to the empty table without looking at Caroline or her beau. Taking his seat, Heck tried to tell himself that she meant nothing to him and had just been an annoying distraction to his plans, but even as he thought it, he knew it was a lie. The more he tried to dismiss his feelings, the madder he grew, even though he knew he had no right to his anger. After all, he and Miss Farber had made no promises to each other.

As he struggled to gain control over his thoughts and emotions, a figure appeared at his table, though the expression she wore was certainly not the one he expected when he rode into Uvalde.

"Hello, Mister Carson," she said coolly.

"So, it's Mister Carson now?"

"I feel it is best that we don't give the appearance of familiarity. I am now spending time with someone else, and it is a small town where the tongues tend to flap rather loosely."

"Yes, I saw the gentleman at your table. His name is Horace Snow, I believe. I would have introduced myself, but I didn't want to interrupt your supper."

"What are you doing here, Heck?" Caroline asked in an annoyed manner that she made no effort to hide.

"I was just passing through on my way to Fredericksburg," he lied, before catching himself. "I came here to see you, of course, but it appears that I have misjudged your feelings, and I will be leaving in the morning."

"It has been six months since I saw you last. You didn't even send word where you were, or even if you were alright. I decided not to wait for you to finally declare your intentions, whatever those might be, and I have pursued other prospects. Since you are to leave tomorrow, I will avoid the massive crowd of well-wishers, and say my farewell now."

Heck knew she was right. He hadn't come around enough and hadn't even granted her the hope of a future. Faced with his own bad behavior, he determined to share the depth of feelings he really felt for her, but before he could speak, Horace Snow walked up behind Caroline.

"Good evening," he said. "My name is Horace Snow, and I don't believe I've had the pleasure."

"I'm Jesse Carson," Heck said, extending his hand.

Turning to Horace, Caroline said, "Mister Carson did a good turn for the town some time back, and he shows up from time to time to bask in their adulation, but he will be leaving us tomorrow."

"I'm sorry to hear that," Horace said. "I'm sure he would be an entertaining dinner companion, but I certainly understand the need for one to go back to where they belong. Caroline, we should really be getting back to our table. The peach pie will be coming shortly."

Resisting his natural tendency to speak his mind, Heck held his tongue and simply wished them both good night. Regardless of his feelings, he was determined to move on the next morning to his brother's ranch. He had no power over the whims of women, but he did have power over his own future.

A good night's sleep in a soft bed did much to rejuvenate his body but did little to heal his spirits. Sheer exhaustion helped sleep come easy, but his dreams were filled with thoughts of her, and things he should have done and said years earlier. He had believed there was plenty of time, he just needed to build a future worthy of her first, but somehow while thinking through his plan, he had forgotten a thing or two.

Standing up and stretching out the muscles that had grown stiff from eight blessed hours of rest, Heck tried to think of something, anything, that he could say to Caroline to win her back, but he realized that he had nothing to offer that Horace Snow couldn't give her in larger measure. After turning it over in his mind a couple hundred times, he concluded that the decision he arrived at the night before in the café was the correct course of action. He would concentrate on building his ranch, and along with it, a sizable fortune for the future.

The food at the hotel wasn't as good as what could be had at the café, but as he finished his eggs and bacon, Heck thought the breakfast was passable and was thankful he'd be able to get out of town without seeing Caroline again.

When his plate was cleaned, and he'd downed his third cup of coffee, he stood up to leave, but was blocked by two very large men, and he was certain they had not come to see him for friendly conversation.

"Morning, boys," Heck said pleasantly. "How can I help y'all?"

"Mister Snow sent us here to be sure you keep your promise about leaving town," one of the men said, moving his coat so that Heck could get a good look at the Colt resting on his hip.

Heck doubted if the man was very fast, but with his size, Heck figured that not many men ever challenged him.

"I appreciate your help, but he didn't have to put y'all through the trouble. I was just finishing my breakfast, and then I was gonna get on my horse and be on my way."

"Glad to hear it, but our orders were to see you leave, so we'll be going with ya."

"Suit yourself, but I guarantee your boss ain't paying ya enough for this," Heck said, pulling his Peacemaker.

Before they could put their hands on their guns, Heck brought the barrel of his pistol down on both men's heads, knocking them to the floor.

The force of steel connecting with bone left both men dazed and unable to regain their feet. Standing over each one, Heck hit them across the bridge of their noses, causing them to cry out in pain. They grabbed their noses, and the sight of blood covering their hands removed any fight the two had left.

Putting his pistol back in his holster, Heck knelt down so that both men could hear what he had to say.

"Tell Horace Snow, the next time he wants to show me where I belong, he'd better do it himself. If I ever see either of you again, I'll bury ya where I find ya."

Heck saddled his horse, and after paying for her feed and board, he rode out of town. He was not one to ever take pleasure in a fight, but as he put Uvalde behind him, the pain he had felt over Caroline was eased somewhat by a sense of satisfaction.

Chapter Ten

The cypress, oak, and pecan trees provided a welcome shade from the sun as Heck's horse maintained a leisurely trot along the bank of the Pedernales River. As he took in the smell of the honeysuckle and listened to the sound of the water flowing gently over the exposed rocks, Heck was returned to the carefree days of his childhood. Memories, as they are apt to do when the years begin to pile up, crept into his mind, like benevolent specters gently pulling him towards the past.

Resisting the grip of the past, Heck returned to the world of the present, and cast a watchful eye over the trail ahead of him and the thick brush on either side. He wasn't usually a man given to daydreaming. Maintaining law along the Texas frontier was an occupation fraught with peril and living in one's thoughts was a habit that a lawman could not afford. He silently cursed himself for giving in to such a worthless indulgence but being in the Hill Country of his youth always had that effect on him.

Other than deer and a few hundred head of cattle, Heck didn't see another soul until he reached the road that cut north from the river. There, he had to pause to allow several wagons to pass, returning the friendly waves of the children riding in the back. Each one seemed to be eagerly anticipating the trip into town, and the break it provided from the daily drudgery of farm and ranch life. As a young boy, he had worn that same expression when he was able to enjoy an adventure away from the lonely monotony of hard work.

Two miles north of the Pedernales, the scrub trees gave way to well-maintained peach orchards, and then to open pasture land. The grass was dotted with roving groups of black cows making their way to and from the ponds of cool water that had been dug on either end of the pasture.

As a boy, Heck had always felt secure on the ranch, surrounded by the beautiful rolling hills, and where the convenience of good water was no further away than the family's well or the Pedernales River. He figured that was why, despite all the adventures he had enjoyed, he was now longing for a spread of his own where he could put down roots and perhaps create that feeling of safety for children of his own.

Guiding his appaloosa on to the hard-packed caliche road that led to the ranch house, he eased his horse to a comfortable trot, glad that only a half mile separated him from the end of his journey.

"Howdy, Heck," Darby called from the front porch of the limestone house.

"Howdy, Darby. I see working for my brother ain't got in the way of your loafing."

"Loafing?" Darby replied. "I just sat down. Jefferson's been working me from sun up to sun down for the last month while you've been out there enjoying yourself in New Mexico. I've been trying to get him to start the drive without ya, just so I could get some rest."

"Your hand don't know much about what happens on a cattle drive if he thinks it's gonna be so restful. Working for you has turned this stray boy into a lazy good for nothing," Jefferson said, stepping from inside the house and onto the porch.

"That's a mouthful from a man that spends every night under a roof and in a soft bed," Heck said with a laugh.

Pulling himself from the rocking chair, Darby said, "Let me take your horse to the barn, so you boys can continue your chat without me."

"Thank ya, Darby," Heck said.

"Don't thank me. If I stick around here much longer, I figure I'll have to break up y'alls fight."

"Be sure she gets some oats and a rub down, and if it comes to a fight between me and my brother, I'm more than capable of finishing it."

"We were just getting ready to eat," Jefferson said, shaking his brother's hand. "I reckon there's enough for one more mouth, if ya ain't already ate."

"You still doing the cooking?" Heck asked.

"That's right. I do the cooking for six men every day, and not one of 'em has complained yet."

"That's good, brother," Heck said. "I'm sure that ain't because all those men draw their wages from you."

"Come see for yourself. The rest of the men should be along any minute."

Heck, Jefferson, Darby, and Jefferson's five ranch hands sat down to a meal of stew and cornbread, and not a word was said between them until the food was devoured. Heck reflected on how good food removed the need for idle conversation, though him and his brother never had that particular problem, good food or not.

After the dishes were cleared and cleaned, Heck and his brother retired to the porch to escape the still stifling heat of the house.

"So, did ya run into a piece of trouble with that outlaw you were tracking?" Jefferson asked, lighting a cigar and passing one to Heck. "We were expecting you over a week ago."

"Yeah, there were a few problems," Heck replied, lighting his own cigar. "I had to save him from some ranchers turned vigilantes. The rancher was an old friend of mine, and I shot up several of his men to save a no-good outlaw."

"I can tell ya as a rancher, that unless you're willing to give into the lawless element, sometimes ya got to deal with the outlaws yourself."

"But not the way they were gonna do it."

"Well, did ya get the man turned over to the law?" Jefferson asked, wondering if Heck really understood that there was a difference between the law and justice.

"No, he ended up getting himself killed anyhow. I reckon a man can't outrun the Lord's judgment."

Jefferson couldn't help but laugh a little at the absurdity of the way things played out. The idea of having to shoot it out with an old friend to save an outlaw, only to have someone else kill him in the end, was certainly worthy of a good laugh. From the look Heck gave him, Jefferson could tell he didn't find the humor in it. "Yeah, that's a bad piece of luck, alright," he said.

Not wanting to talk about it any further, Heck looked out into the darkness, and let the conversation lag. He blew small ringlets of bluish-gray smoke, enjoying the rich flavor of the fine cigar as he basked in the peaceful sounds of nature.

"The pasture sure is green. You must have gotten some good rain this year," Heck said, finally breaking the silence.

"The Lord has blessed us lately, that's for sure. The river's up by two feet as well, so I've been grazing a few hundred head down in the lower forty. They should be a good weight for making the trip north."

"It'll be a rough trip, though," Heck said. "The ones that make the drive will have to be sturdy,"

"They're Santa Gertrudis cows from the King Ranch. Captain King swears by their hearty nature and stamina, so I made a deal with him for two hundred head. They should make the trip in good shape and will crossbreed well with your stock."

Heck was not the expert in cows that his brother was, so he just nodded his head in agreement. If this new breed was good enough for Jefferson and Richard King, he certainly wasn't going to disagree. "That's good thinking, Jeff. That's why I need your help getting my ranch going, cause you know about such things."

"I'm happy to help, but I ain't taking you on to raise. Don't forget, I've got a ranch of my own to run."

"I know," Heck replied, "and you've done a great job around here. It's never looked this good, even when Pa was running it."

Taking one last puff from his cigar, Jefferson crushed it out under his boot. "I don't know how ya do things on your ranch, but around here, we start work before sun up, so we should get some sleep. There's a lot of work to be done before we head north."

Chapter Eleven

Heck, Jefferson and Darby spent four days preparing for the cattle drive. They branded calves, rotated stock to the richer grass along the river, and cutout the two hundred head that would be making the drive to Heck's ranch. Since Jefferson would be in North Texas for several months helping his brother, there was much maintenance to do so that the few hands he was leaving behind would be able to concentrate on working the cows and horses. They mended fences, repaired the roof on both the barn and house, and they stocked the loft with plenty of hay for the winter.

"We leave at first light, boys, so you'd better turn in early," Jefferson said, clearing the supper dishes.

"You don't have to tell me twice," Darby said. "I've been working so hard since I set foot on this ranch, that I'm asleep before my head hits the pillow."

"I know what ya mean, kid," Heck chimed in. "If we spend another day here, my brother will have us building him a new house."

"Pardon me," Jefferson said. "Here I thought I was traveling hundreds of miles to drive my cows to your ranch, but apparently it's you that's been put upon. Never mind that while I'm up north, everything I've built here will be going to seed."

"Don't worry, I'll pay ya for the beeves, and just remember, it was your idea to crossbreed my stock with these special cows of yours."

"I know, that's what I get for letting my generous nature get the better of me, and you dang sure will pay me back. Neither one of us is gonna get what we want if those cows don't make it up north, and I can promise you, it will be no easy journey."

By the time the golden rays of the morning began streaking down the hills to kiss the dew, Heck, Darby, and Jefferson were moving north through a deep valley, with two hundred head of cattle and twenty wild mustangs.

Even though Heck and Jefferson had carefully plotted their route, the first day on the trail was plagued by unforeseen tribulations. Several felled trees blocked their path and had to be removed. Heavy rains had caused the local creeks to become swollen, which made for treacherous crossings, and all three men were soaked to the bone by the time they made their first camp. It soon became evident to the men that they had been overly confident in the miles they would be able to move per day.

Forgotten Country   John Spiars

Moving a herd, even a small one such as theirs, was an almost impossible task for three men. One man was always having to break off to retrieve strays, leaving the other two with the task of pushing the herd forward.

They took turns standing watch over the cows at night, and each day that man would have to spend all day in the saddle without the benefit of sleep. Each morning, the three men would draw straws to see who would be riding drag, and unlucky indeed was the man who pulled watch and then had to spend the next day eating dust at the back of the herd.

Collapsing to the ground in front of the fire, Heck took a long draw from his canteen, and seldom had water ever tasted sweeter. The days dirt had collected in his throat, making it both hard to breathe and talk.

"I swear I've pulled drag every day since we started," Heck said, coughing up dust with each word.

"At least we're saving food since you're eating trail dust for every meal," Jefferson said, getting a hearty belly laugh from Darby.

Heck pulled two strips of salted pork from the fire and filled his plate with the beans that Jefferson had cooked in a thick, brown gravy.

"We'll be hitting the lower Brazos tomorrow," Heck said, "so I think I should scout ahead a few miles first thing in the morning. It'll make an easy day for you two, as y'all can just keep moving behind me at a leisurely pace."

"That's probably a good idea," Jefferson said, "though I don't like the thought of you missing out on a day's work. You might just decide to chuck it all and ride off on another one of your adventures."

"I might at that. After a week of riding with you two, chasing Indians and outlaws don't sound half bad."

Before sun up, Heck rose, ate a quick breakfast and packed his horse with two days' worth of provisions. The cows were beginning to meander about, munching on the plentiful grass, obviously awaiting the signal to get on the move.

"You sure are taking a lot of supplies for just one day," Darby said, riding into camp from his night watching over the herd. "You are coming back to the drive, ain't ya?"

"He ain't made up his mind yet," Jefferson said, as he reluctantly climbed out of his bed roll. "I reckon driving cows is more work than he's interested in. He'd rather go straight to being a cattle baron."

"Dang it, Jeff," Heck said, "you've been on me since we was kids, and it's beginning to wear thin. One of us has to ride ahead to scout the river crossing. We need you to stay with the herd in case of problems, so that just leaves me to do the scouting, unless you wanna trust your life to Darby."

"What do ya mean by that?" Darby said, warming his insides with a cup of coffee. "I can find the river just as good as either one of you."

"You might be able to find the Brazos, but you'd pick a crossing that would get the whole lot of us drowned," Heck said, placing his rifle in its scabbard. "You take care of the heavy work and leave the thinking to me and Jefferson."

Darby knew that Heck was only joshing him, but he didn't want him to think that he enjoyed it. "I've been up all night guarding your cows. What have you been doing?"

Forgotten Country   John Spiars

"I made coffee and fried the bacon," Heck said. "It looks like Jefferson is the only one that's been loafing this morning."

"Don't you get me involved in y'alls morning spat," Jefferson said, as he poured himself a cup of coffee. "Y'all are missing out on the best part of cowboying, being able to be off by yourself and not having to spend your time yacking."

With dawn breaking over the trees, Heck climbed into the saddle and prepared to ride off. "I'm gonna leave y'all to work out that argument amongst yourselves, and I'll meet ya at the river."

"Keep your eyes open out there," Jefferson said seriously. "There ain't too many Indians left in these parts, but I've heard that Quanah and his band might be this far south."

"You do the same, brother," Heck replied, touching his spurs lightly to his appaloosa's side.

As the sound of the cows faded away, Heck's well-developed sense of danger took over. He thought about Jefferson's words of warning, though they were hardly news to Heck. Most of the Comanche leaders had surrendered and been moved to reservations in Indian Territory, but not Quanah and his band. They had recently been responsible for attacks on buffalo hunters in the Panhandle, and some had claimed to have seen roaming bands of Comanche much further south. He figured most of those claims were just people spinning a yarn, but the possibility of crossing paths with a raiding party kept Heck alert to every sound.

Heck's hope of reaching the Brazos River in less than a day were dashed as the hours flew by far quicker than the miles. Every time he thought he must be getting close, his path would open up into a vast prairie, or take him into a dense forest, where even the fading light of dusk didn't reach.

Never one to travel after dark through unknown terrain, Heck reluctantly decided to make camp. He found a small clearing nestled in the midst of the towering oaks, and after making a ring of stones, he built a small fire and cooked a few pieces of bacon. To satisfy his sweet tooth, he sprinkled some sugar in the bacon grease and fried up one of the apples he carried in his saddlebag. It wasn't the best meal he had ever eaten, but it filled his belly, and as he washed it down with a cup of strong coffee, he had to admit, it was pretty darn good.

Heck chose a spot where the tree branches hung close to the ground to spread out his bed roll. They would shield him from view and protect him from any weather that might move in on him.

He had only been asleep for a short time, still in that netherworld where reality mixed with the world of dreams, when the sound of distant gunfire snatched him from peaceful sleep.

Chapter Twelve

Through the fog of half-consciousness, Heck's instincts took control, and instead of jumping up and running headlong into the unknown, he remained still and listened for any signs of approaching danger.

The sound of rifle and pistol fire continued for several more seconds, and whatever was happening, Heck knew that someone was fighting for their life, though he could tell the trouble was at least a mile away.

The lawman in him wanted to ride out and lend a hand, but in the middle of the night, he realized he would be entering a dangerous situation totally blind, and that's how more than a few good lawmen found an early grave. Instead, he doused the campfire, hunkered down with his rifle pulled close, and waited for the light of day.

Forgotten Country   John Spiars

Between listening for the sounds of anyone approaching his camp, Heck managed to get a few hours of sleep. Years of living outdoors in hostile territory had given him the ability to sleep for short periods of time while still being able to stay alert for any sign of approaching trouble. It was a valuable skill to have, but one that took years to develop, and many a young lawman met his maker before ever acquiring it.

It wasn't any sound that woke Heck up just before dawn, but a smell. A stiff, westerly breeze carried the scent of burning wood. As he stood to work out the stiffness caused by sleeping on the hard ground, the faint hint of smoke burned his eyes. Wood wasn't the only smell that caught Heck's attention, he also recognized the unmistakable scent of burning flesh.

Quickly breaking camp, he mounted his appaloosa and rode off to the west, and towards an unknown danger.

A quarter mile ride brought Heck out of the dense woods and to the bottom of a small hill, where a narrow creek snaked off towards the north. Finding a spot where the bank sloped gently down to the creek bed, he splashed through the shallow water and back up the other side. As he leaned over his horse's neck to make the climb up the opposite bank, it occurred to him that the creek undoubtedly fed into the Brazos, and no more than a mile or two to the north.

Leaving the creek, he crossed an open grassland at the end of which was a small rise, where wisps of black smoke were still rising from the burned-out remnants of a small stone house.

Heck pulled the spyglass from his saddlebag and slowly moved it from left to right, looking for any signs that those responsible were still about. He saw that the house was almost completely burned except for the limestone shell, and the dried grass around the structures was blackened from the fire as well.

Seeing no signs of life, Heck laid his Henry across his lap and made his way up the dirt path. Along the way, he kept his ears and eyes open for any sign of an attack.

At the top of the little mound, the stench of flesh assaulted his nose, and the swirling smoke stung his eyes. He covered his mouth and nose with his bandana, but his eyes were left exposed and began watering to the point that it became hard to see.

Walking his horse around the property, he saw that it was indeed Comanche who had attacked the farm. Hoof prints of unshod horses covered the ground, as well as several arrows, though it appeared that some attempt had been made to cover their tracks. In the darkness, it had probably become a futile effort to mask their trail, and Heck saw where at least ten horses had ridden off to the north.

With no sign of impending danger, Heck dismounted and entered the charred remains of the house. Being careful where he walked, he stepped over pieces of blackened wood and remnants of household goods and furniture. Along the back wall was the sickening sight he knew he would find, the earthly remains of three bodies. Two were adult and one was a child, though it was impossible to tell if they were men or women.

Carrying his rifle at the ready, Heck stepped from the hellish scene of death, into the welcoming sunlight. He walked fifty yards to the barn, whose doors were standing open, and seemed to be completely unscathed from the destruction of the attackers. A quick walk through the small structure revealed it to be completely empty of life.

Forgotten Country   John Spiars

The animals that had once been contained within were now the property of the Comanche.

Stepping back into the daylight, Heck caught sight of someone running from the edge of the yard into the trees. Heck shouldered his rifle and aimed the barrel at the tree line, in case the runner was a scout for a war party, but detecting no further movement, he ran to where he had ground tied his horse and rode off in pursuit of the stranger.

Riding through the thick brush, Heck had to use his rifle barrel to move the thin limbs that clogged the narrow game trail. Whoever the person was, they were moving along in a hurry and appeared to have much experience traversing the local terrain. The person made no effort to cover their trail or even change directions, which was a sure sign that they were running out of fear and not as part of a planned attack.

Nudging his appaloosa to a quick walk, Heck kept his head moving, watching both the trail in front of him and the dense thorny brush on either side. As he picked up the pace, he could hear the crushing of leaves in front of him and realized that the person was only a few feet ahead.

"Whoever you are, you ain't gotta be afraid. I came to help," Heck called, spurring his horse to a trot.

The dirt path suddenly sloped into a deep ravine and Heck saw his quarry tumble down the ten-foot slope, flipping feet over head until reaching the bottom, where he was swallowed up by the thick carpet of leaves that covered the ground.

"You alright?" Heck called from the top of the incline.

Slowly a figure rose from the ground, partially covered in leaves, and looking for someplace to run. Heck kept his rifle pointed at the bottom of the ravine but was reasonably sure he had nothing to fear from the leaf covered specter.

After spitting out leaves and dusting off the dirt and foliage, a teenage boy emerged from underneath, appearing to be no more than sixteen years old. Seeing that there was nowhere to run, but not trusting the man who had been chasing him, the boy just stood silently staring back at Heck.

"Are ya alright, son?"

"I—I think so," the boy said. "Ya ain't gotta hurt me mister. I got nothing to steal, and I don't want no trouble."

"I ain't gonna hurt ya, kid. My name's Heck, and I was camping about a mile from here when I heard the trouble. Was that your home back yonder?"

"Yeah, I lived there with my folks and sister."

"What's your name?"

"Orville Digsby, but most folks call me Digger."

"Well, Digger, ya think you can climb out of that ditch?"

"I think so," Digger said, sliding on the slick earth as he tried to pull himself from the ravine.

"Good," Heck said. "Then we'll work on getting out of these brambles you led us into."

After the boy finally made it back to solid ground, Heck lifted him into the saddle behind him, and they rode through the thorny brush, back to the smoldering ruins that had once been Digger's home.

"You wanna tell me what happened here?" Heck asked, as the boy slid off the horse.

Looking at the blackened grass and the crumbling skeleton that had once been his family's house, Digger seemed for a moment as if he might cry. He meandered about the yard for a while, as if lost, searching for the life he had known, but in an instant, he caught himself and wiped a stray tear from his eye.

"I had already gone to bed. I only woke up when my pa come into the room and told me and my sister to hide under the bed. From our hiding place, we could hear yelping and screaming from outside, and my pa shooting from the front room. Sis was so scared. She climbed from under the bed and ran out of the room, but I didn't move."

Digger's breath came in short gasps as he told the story, and he had to stop several times to regain his voice.

"I heard 'em break through the door, and then there was more screaming and a couple more shots. After that, it got real quiet, the quietest I ever heard. Pretty soon, I heard the crackling of fire and the whole house filled with smoke. I figured I'd die under that bed and then we'd all be together again, but I woke up when I heard you walking around. After you went to the barn, I climbed out and just started running."

Heck had heard the same story before. The people were different, but the stories were almost always identical. Having been friendly with several Comanche, Heck understood their plight, and figured given the same circumstances, he would act in much the same way, but hearing stories like Diggers still provoked a deep anger in him toward the Indians.

Digger sat down where the front porch had once been and stared out toward the open field where a crop would be coming up in a few months. The view from that direction gave no hint of the devastation that had transpired, and Heck could almost hear the denial playing out in the young man's head.

"I've got to tend to your family now," Heck said, walking past Digger. "You just sit here till I'm done."

Digger stood up and began to follow Heck. "I can help ya."

"No, you stay here. You don't wanna remember your family like this. Besides, I've had a lot of practice at this sort of thing, and I've gotten to where I can do it pretty quick."

The afternoon heat bore down as Heck finished burying Digger's family and sapped what little strength he had left. The oppressive humidity made the air so thick that it could almost be cut with a knife, and as he sat next to Digger, he took a long drink from his canteen before offering it to the boy.

"Do ya have any more kin in these parts?" Heck asked, as Digger continued to stare toward the eastern horizon.

"Nah," he replied. "My folks come to Texas from Missouri. I heard 'em talk a few times about family there, but I don't even remember their names."

"Are there any friends or neighbors around that would take ya in?"

"We don't know that many people, and the few we do know are having a hard time feeding the mouths they already have. It's alright though, the barn's still standing, and I can live in there for a spell, at least till I can build the house back. I should have a good crop this fall, and that will give me some money to get by on."

Thinking about the situation, Heck shook his head. "Building a house and bringing in a crop sounds like a big load for one man. I've got a ranch up in North Texas, and my brother and me are driving some cattle up there. There are just three of us and we could surely use some more help. I could pay ya a dollar a day plus found, and I'd also throw in a horse for ya. What do ya think?"

"It sure sounds better than staying here by myself," Digger said. "Ya think we might run into those Indians who attacked us?"

"Likely not," Heck replied. "They're on the run from the Army and will probably make their way out west where they can hide out for a while."

Heck didn't really believe what he told the kid, but the boy needed to make peace with his loss and not be driven by the need for vengeance. Heck knew a thing or two about that.

"You can sit behind me on my horse till we cross paths with my brother. It shouldn't take more than a few hours, but we best get started."

Heck and Digger only had to ride a few miles before they came upon Jefferson and Darby pressing forward with the herd. Heck could tell by the look of both men that they had a hard go moving the cows by themselves, and he figured he would hear about it soon enough from his brother. He wasn't disappointed.

"Where have ya been?" Jefferson called out, once Heck was within shouting distance. "We expected ya back a half day ago. We might as well have chewed our own way."

"Dang it, Jefferson. Don't I even a get a 'How'd do,' before ya start hollering at me?"

"Who's that on the saddle with ya?" Jefferson asked, after seeing the boy.

"His name's Digger, and he just signed on with us."

"I see. I didn't know we was taking on hands, and children at that."

"He might not look like much, but ya ought to see him run. The kid can light a shuck like nothing ya ever seen."

"Is he gonna run all the way to the ranch?" Darby asked, eyeing the boy suspiciously.

"No, I want you to set him up with a horse outta our string. The sorrel should work good for him. I'm putting him with ya till he learns the ropes."

"Ya think I ain't got nothing better to do than to take on a green kid?" Darby said.

"From the looks of you boys, it seems ya could use the help moving these cows along, and I figure I can cut your wages in order to pay him."

"The kids had a hard break, that's sure enough, but that don't mean we gotta take him on as our responsibility," Jefferson said, after Heck explained the circumstances of how he found Digger.

"What would ya have me do, just leave him there where I found him? He needs our help, and the truth is, we could use another hand on this drive. After we get back, we'll figure things out."

"Did ya at least find the river crossing ya went to look for?"

"Not exactly," Heck said, sheepishly bowing his head. "The river's only a few miles ahead. There's an open field that skirts the trees, and it should lead right down to the water. Once there, I'll find us a good spot to cross."

"What about those Comanche? Any chance well run into 'em on the way?"

"I doubt it," Heck said. "Quanah's trying to make a show to the Army by striking this far south, but he wants to keep his band together, not lose 'em in a battle with troops. I figure he took some scalps and horses and now he's looking to get back to his range along the Red River. Besides, as slow as we're moving, they'd get tired of waiting on us, even if they were lying in wait to attack."

"I hope ya know what you're doing," Jefferson said, shaking his head.

"I usually don't, but things always seem to work out in the end. I reckon I'm blessed that way."

"Well, I've heard tell that the Lord takes special care over drunks and fools, and I reckon you fit the bill for at least one of those," Jefferson said. Shaking his head, he set spur to horse and rode on, muttering something under his breath, though Heck couldn't quite make out what it was.

Once they reached the Brazos, the water wasn't too deep, but was running downstream at a brisk pace.

"I don't like the looks of it," Jefferson said, "but I don't reckon we got much choice but to cross."

Heck watched the water rushing by and didn't like the idea of fording such swift water any better than Jefferson. "I reckon I could scout up river a piece, but it might just be a waste of time."

Studying on it a minute, Jefferson said, "I say we just make the best of it and try to cross. We've lost enough time on this drive as it is."

"The river narrows about a mile downstream, and will make an easier crossing," Digger said.

"Are ya sure about that, son?" Jefferson asked, not at all confident in their new hand.

"Of course, I'm sure. I've crossed it a hundred times on my horse, and my pa's done it twice that many, a few times with our plowing mule. It's so narrow ya can almost jump across."

The spot was just as Digger had promised. Maybe not quite an easy jump, but they got the cows across it easily just the same.

"I do believe that boy of yours is lucky for us," Jefferson said, smiling as he watched the herd climb up the short bank on the north side of the Brazos.

"He'll work out just fine," Heck said. "He might be a farmer, but he's got the knack for driving cows. Did ya see the way he went after those stragglers?"

"Darby better watch out he don't lose his job to that kid," Jefferson said with a laugh.

A renewed feeling of confidence came over the men as they brought their cows into a green pasture that seemed to stretch on for miles. Flat, green carpets of wild Texas grass spread out before them, a welcome sight since they needed a place to bed the herd down for the night. They could spend the night and the following day there, allowing the animals to graze freely and put on some of the weight they had already lost on the long walk.

The good mood among the drovers didn't last long and was quickly replaced by one of dread. Searching the horizon for any sign of danger, Heck peered through his spyglass, but what he found was more trouble than he had expected. Less than a mile directly in front of them were five Comanche warriors on painted horses waiting for Heck's group to ride into their grasp.

Chapter Thirteen

The Comanche braves watched from the high ground but showed no sign of attack. Heck and the others halted the cows in the poorly defensible open ground, with only a hundred yards of grassland separating them from the enemy.

"Maybe they don't plan to attack us at all," Darby said hopefully. "You said that it was probably fifteen that attacked that boy's ranch."

"Oh, they're gonna attack, alright, but I can't figure out what they're waiting for," Jefferson said, as he looked through his own field glass.

"They want us to make the first move," Heck replied. "They hold the high ground and know they can ride down on us from any direction once we make our move."

"Where do ya think the others are?" Jefferson asked.

"More than likely they're making their way north and sent these braves to cover their back trail. It would be considered quite a feat if the five of 'em were able to take this herd."

Through his field glass, Heck saw that the five warriors were painted with black and white stripes running down their faces. It was the war paint of the Quahadi band, whose leader was the half white Quanah Parker. Their horses were splashed with streaks of red and yellow color and decorated with rings of eagle feathers around their necks.

Quanah and his band were the last Comanche holdouts along the "Staked Plains," refusing to be moved to Indian Territory. For the last several years they had been fighting a protracted war of attrition against the U.S. Army, making lightning strikes against remote and poorly defended outposts. Their main target had been the buffalo hunters who were decimating the herds that had roamed along the Red River and into the Panhandle. The wild buffalo herds had been the source of food, clothing, tools and weapons for the Comanche for hundreds of years and served as much of a spiritual purpose as they did a practical one. Quanah realized it was a war he wouldn't win, but it was a point of honor with him and his men, so the losses they incurred made little difference in the balance of it all.

"If they're waiting for us to make a move, we'd better make it a good one," Jefferson said, drawing his Walker Colt.

"And so, we shall," Heck said, placing his spyglass back in his saddlebag.

"You have a plan?" Jefferson asked.

"I do, but you're not going to like it."

"They're gonna kill all of us, and there ain't nothing we can do about it," Digger said, a look of terror evident in his eyes.

"The kid's got a point," Darby replied. "We're easy pickings out here in the open."

"What's your plan, Heck?" Jefferson asked.

"The Comanche want two things, us and the herd. Let's just give 'em one and see what happens. We'll stampede the herd in their direction and see if they'll go after them."

"We're just gonna let 'em have the cows?"

"I ain't letting 'em have anything. If they go after the herd they'll lose the high ground, and the odds will be even."

Heck reached back into his saddlebags and pulled out his old Walker Colt. After quickly checking the loads, he rode over and handed it to Digger.

"Have you ever used a pistol before?"

"No," Digger replied. "Pa taught me to use a rifle, and we'd go hunting together. He let me take a big buck last year."

"I don't want ya to shoot unless you have to. If you have to shoot, pull back the hammer like this, and pull the trigger. You'll have six shots, so make 'em count. Try to stay behind me, and don't get yourself shot."

"Well, let's do this," Jefferson said.

Heck and Jefferson rode to the back of the herd, and from either side, they fired their pistols into the air, driving the cows forward. The startled animals took off across the open range towards the rise where the Comanche braves patiently waited. Running at full speed, the horses and cows created a thunderous racket as their hooves pounded the earth.

As the running animals approached their position, the Comanche showed no sign of taking the bait, and Heck feared he had misjudged his foe. He tried coming up with an alternate plan, but he determined that if the original one failed, the only other option left to the group was the uncertainty of pitched battle on open ground, and Heck didn't like the odds of success in such a fight.

When the herd passed just below their position, the braves, unable to resist the opportunity for such a prize, turned their horses and rode down from their perch.

The five Comanches made their way down the hill at a fast trot, so seizing the chance, Heck pulled his Henry and lined up one of the warriors in his sights. He judged his shot carefully, led his target slightly to allow for wind, and gently squeezed the trigger.

Heck always hated the idea of killing a man without giving them the chance to surrender, but in this case, he put these feelings aside. They were facing an enemy who were more than willing to kill, and he knew he had to take any opportunity to reduce their number.

Heck's shot was true and struck the warrior in the chest, knocking him off his horse. Not wanting to lose the advantage, he spurred his horse to a run and raced after the herd, followed by Jefferson, Darby and Digger.

The green earth passed by in a blur beneath the hooves of their horses as Heck and the others pursued the Comanche. The herd of cows and horses were several hundred yards in front of them, with the Comanche braves riding alongside, trying to control their panicked frenzy.

As Heck closed the distance to the runaway herd, he saw that the Comanche's efforts to turn the cows was to no avail. They fired their pistols furiously and slapped at the animals with their ropes in an attempt to try and direct the beasts, but despite a valiant effort, the herd began to scatter in all directions.

As he bared down on the warriors, Heck began firing his rifle with one hand and held his reins with the other, careful not to hit his horses or cows.

Giving up on taking the herd, two of the Indians broke off the chase and rode off to the northeast, while the other two turned their paint horses around and galloped towards Heck.

The Comanche were known as the best horsemen on the Plains, and the Quahadi were the best of the bunch, so Heck chose to take away their advantage. Pulling on the reins, Heck turned his horse's head to the left, bringing her to a sudden stop. He quickly leapt to the ground, shouldered his Henry, and flipped up the ladder sites, drawing a bead on the approaching Comanche.

Taking a deep breath, he slowly exhaled and waited for his foe to get closer before gently squeezing the trigger. The bullet tore through the brave's mid-section causing him to drop the reins, but he managed to stay on the animals back for a few moments. He raised his pistol and fired two shots that whizzed by Heck's ear before his strength gave out and he tumbled to the ground.

Seeing his fellow warrior lying dead in the dirt appeared to have no effect on the other brave as he thundered past the body and straight at Heck.

Heck shifted his rifle barrel to the left and lined the man up in his sites, but before he could fire, Digger rode between him and the Indian. Reluctantly, Heck lowered his weapon and watched as Digger and the Comanche rode at each other in what would be a fight to the death.

Digger handled his horse better than most seasoned cowboys as he galloped across the prairie firing the Walker

Colt. Even an expert gunhand would have fared poorly in a shooting fight on horseback against a Comanche brave, and Digger was certainly no expert. The forty-four pistol was too powerful for a sixteen-year-old boy to handle with one hand, and his shots were nowhere close to their mark.

Heck watched as the two men rode to within twenty feet of each other, certain that he would see the boy fall at any moment. The Comanche's shots had all went wide, but Heck knew that the warrior's experience would win out eventually, and end in the kid's death.

Digger wasn't sure how many shots he had fired but figured he had only one or two remaining and cursed himself for not being a better shot. He drew in a deep breath to steady himself and adjusted his aim down and a little to his left. Digger then drew the hammer back and held his shot until he was within just a few feet of colliding with his enemy's horse. As his index finger tightened around the trigger and prepared to squeeze, he was sure he could smell the sweat pouring off the warrior's body and realized that the man had his pistol pointed directly at his head. Seeing he was out of time, Digger pulled the reins to the right and fired his pistol. Turning around in the saddle, he saw the Comanche's horse topple forward, and the warrior fly over its head. The brave hit the ground hard, rolled a few times, and then came to rest some twenty feet away.

With his rifle shouldered, Heck ran to where the Indian lay motionless and checked the man for any signs of life, but he found none.

"Is he dead?" Jefferson asked, riding up next to Heck.

"He's dead, alright," Heck replied, "and so is his horse. The kid don't mess around, that's for sure."

"What about the other two?"

"I don't reckon we'll see them again. They had the good sense to live to fight another day."

"Did I get him," Digger called, as he reined his horse to a stop. "I got him, didn't I? I knew I did."

"You got him, kid," Heck said. Reaching into his saddlebag, he pulled out his spyglass and began scanning the horizon. "It looks like we've got our work cut out for us, boys. There ain't a cow or horse in sight. Let's get these poor fellas planted and round up our herd."

"We ain't really gonna take the time to bury these savages, are we?" Digger said with disgust.

"They're not savages, kid. They were men just like us, but with a different set of beliefs. We did what we had to do, and they did what they had to do. The only difference is, we get to see another day, but tomorrow that could be us and that's something worth thinking about. I know what they've taken from ya, son, but hate is like a poison. It'll eat at your insides till there's nothing left and then you'll be just as good as dead. I'm sure your folks wouldn't want that for you. We'll bury 'em over yonder."

After digging graves for the three Comanches, the men split into two groups to find the herd. Darby and Digger headed north, while Heck and Jefferson rode to the west.

"That boys got some powerful hate working inside him," Jefferson said, as the two plodded along the desolate grassland.

"His whole family was butchered by the Comanche. I'd be carrying some hate myself. I just hope some of what I said took hold."

"I know what you're saying, but you saw how he went after that Indian. He charged right at him without any fear and didn't give it a second thought after killing him."

"What I saw was a boy who put his fear aside to do what needed doin'. That boy will go far, mark my words."

"Maybe so," Jefferson said, not convinced by Heck's words. "If he don't get himself killed or end up swinging from a rope."

"Look over there," Heck said, pointing to some dark forms in the distance.

Jefferson looked through his field glass and saw a large group of cows grazing on the tall grass. "Those are our cows, alright. I count maybe fifty to sixty head, but no horses."

"Well, it's a start," Heck said. "We've only been looking for less than an hour, so there's still hope we'll find the others."

Not wanting to spook the cows, Heck and Jefferson approached them from different directions, and slowly nudged them along to the west. The hungry animals were not anxious to have their meal interrupted, but with a little encouragement, they fell in behind a leader and reluctantly moved as they were directed.

Driving the cattle, the two men made slow time, and the sun was quickly sinking below the horizon when they came across seven horses in a shallow draw. The horses were pacing back and forth along a dry creek bed, lapping up the water that had pooled in several spots among the large rocks.

Heck watched the horses for some time to judge which one was considered the leader, and then rode into the draw and got his rope around the animal's neck. As he led the large roan across the creek bed to the other side, the others watched for a few seconds, and then obediently fell into a trot behind them.

Forgotten Country   John Spiars

With sixty-two cows and seven horses, the two men would not be able to stop for sleep, so they chose to keep riding and look for more strays.

After two days in the saddle, Heck and Jefferson had found seventy-eight cows and eleven horses, but as they were both exhausted, they decided to turn back to meet up with the others. They kept moving day and night, taking cat naps as they rode, and only stopped for short periods so the animals could graze and rest.

"I hope them other boys found the rest of the cows and horses or this will be one costly drive," Jefferson said, straining to keep his eyes open.

"We should've gone further west; we might have found more of our cows," Heck said.

"We're both about to fall out of the saddle as it is, and besides, any of them that made it that far are too stupid to breed."

"This whole experience is enough to sour a man on cowboying, that's for sure. If we don't meet up with the others soon, I'm just gonna drop and make my home wherever I fall."

Jefferson chuckled at his brother's complaining. "This ain't nothing. A few Indians, some lost cows, dang brother, I've been on drives a whole lot worse than this. During the war, I moved a herd to Missouri for our boys, fighting our way through hostile Comanche and Union troops the whole way. When we finally made it, all we had to show for our trouble was two cows that were nothing but skin and bones, and that was still more meat than them Rebs had seen in months. This is a church social compared to that drive."

Five days after parting ways, Heck and Jefferson crested a grassy mound, and below them, nestled along a small pond, were Darby and Digger, keeping watch over more than a hundred cows and seven horses.

"What do ya think of that?" Jefferson said, with a huge grin on his face. "Those boys might just make cowmen after all."

"That sight might be as close to Heaven as we get here on earth," Heck said.

Smelling the water and sweet grass, the herd began pawing at the ground, trying to push their way down the hill. Spurring his horse lightly, Heck guided them to the bottom, and then let them have their head so they could drink and eat as they pleased.

"We was beginning to wonder if you fellas was coming back," Darby said, starting a large campfire next to the water. "Me and the kid were about to divvy up the cows and go into business for ourselves."

"How long have you boys been here?" Jefferson asked, climbing off his horse and sticking his head into the clear water.

"Three days, give or take. We found the animals on the first day and it took us two more to find this place. It's about as pretty as any place ya ever saw, ain't it. We figured y'all would find us sooner or later, and if ya didn't, well, we figured there were worse places to call home."

Collapsing into the soft grass, Heck looked out over what was left of the herd and gave thanks to his God for seeing them through their recent trial. As he lay there, exhausted beyond anything he had ever felt, he watched Digger working the cows like he was born to it. He kept the animals together, and the minute one started to stray, he was on them, nudging them back into the fold.

"Digger seems to be getting the hang of it," Heck said, rubbing his eyes.

Darby nodded his head and said, "That boy didn't sleep for three days, not till we found this place and he was sure I'd had my forty winks. I ain't never seen a man ride for the brand like that kid."

"You might have yourself a ranch, after all," Jefferson said. "For sure, you've got some good hands here."

"No," Heck said, "We'll have a ranch. We're partners, remember."

Chapter Fourteen

Battered by weeks on the trail and their many trials, the Carson brothers, along with Darby and Digger, dragged themselves and their herd along the dusty road that led to their new home.

Looking over the vast expanse of pasture land, Heck felt great pride, though at the moment, he bore a closer resemblance to a shifty vagabond than a would-be cattle baron.

"We'll put the herd in the small pasture for now," Heck said.

"Is this really your ranch?" Digger asked, his eyes as big as saucers. As he gazed about the boundless sea of green that stretched from horizon to horizon, he couldn't believe anyone could own that much land.

"This is part of it. Actually, we've been on the ranch for the last hour. See that rise over yonder, just beyond the river? A few years back, a couple of men were driving a small herd up north, when they were set on by a Comanche war party. They made it to that rise and held them Indians off for three days. When they finally made it out, them cowboys named it Paradise Ridge. Don't just consider this a ranch, Digger. It's your home for as long as you want it."

"I bet Ulley has given us up for dead," Darby said.

"I just hope he ain't forsaken his chores for the bottle entirely," Heck replied, unlatching the gate to the east pasture.

After settling the herd near the creek that ran along the bottom of the grassland, Heck led the way up the winding drive toward the house.

Jefferson took in the ranch the way only a working cowboy could. He looked at the easy source of fresh water, the quality of grass, and the sturdiness of the stock. It wasn't all blue skies and sunshine, but Jefferson figured it was enough to work with. "I gotta admit, I wasn't expecting much from this ranch of yours, but it might just amount to something after all."

"It's our ranch, brother, and we'll make it the finest spread in North Texas."

Arriving at the house, the group was greeted by Ulley, who was seated on the long porch, a half-empty bottle cradled in his arm.

"Damnation," he exclaimed. "I'd given you boys up for dead. Everybody's been talking about how Quanah's boys are on the war path, so I figured we'd find your butchered bones along the trail."

Forgotten Country									John Spiars

"I can see you've worked yourself into quite a state of fear, but it seems you've at least kept the ranch afloat in my absence," Heck said, passing a glaring eye at the bottle in his foreman's hand. "C'mon boys, let's get these horses bedded down in the barn and see if we can rustle up something to fortify ourselves, assuming we got something around here besides whiskey."

"I've got beans and cornbread on the stove, but hadn't ya better introduce me to the new fellas first?"

"I'll introduce ya, but the way you're going at that bottle, I'll just have to repeat myself in the morning. The kid here's named Digger, and this is my brother, Jefferson."

"Good to meet you fellas. My name's Ulley. I don't know where y'all are gonna sleep, cause we only got three beds, but welcome to the, uh, Heck, have you come up with a name for this place yet?"

"No, but as soon as I get a moment where I ain't getting shot at or traipsing across the country looking for strays, I'll sit down and come up with a name for ya. Now, if you're done talking, I'd like to get some feed for my horse and then get some for myself."

Taking a swig from his bottle, Ulley shook his head and said, "Go on then. You leave me here for months by myself and then you don't even give me the courtesy of conversation. I'll get some coffee going, but you new fellers are gonna have to sleep on the floor."

By the time Heck woke up the next morning, the sun was already up, and he caught the unmistakable smell of bacon frying. He'd had a late supper, so he wasn't all that hungry, but the smell of bacon had a way of enticing a man, even if he wasn't in a mood to eat.

Heck rolled out of bed and took a moment to work out the stiffness in his back. Weeks in the saddle left his body aching, though he could remember a time when he could spend a year on the trail and jump out of bed ready for more. Somewhere along the way, he'd traded a sore back for the wisdom that came with age, but on mornings like this, he figured he'd rather have the spryness of youth.

"Morning," Ulley said, as he tended to the bacon and eggs. "I was beginning to wonder if ya was gonna get up or not."

"Where is everyone?" Heck asked, pouring a cup of coffee.

"Your brother and the boy are taking a ride around the ranch. Jefferson said he wanted to see what he got himself into. Darby's still sleeping. That brother of yours sure is a go-getter."

"Yeah, he got all the gumption in the family. He'll get this place into shape and keep you boys in line to boot."

"What do ya mean? I'd say I've done a fair job keeping things running, and without any help."

Heck looked out the window as the sun reflected off the deep grass. "You've held things together pretty good. It seems ya even learned how to cook some in my absence."

"It's a dang good thing I did too, otherwise, I wouldn't have even had the strength to hold a bottle by now. Them outlaws you took out after must've given you boys a run for your money."

"It didn't go easy, that's for sure. We also crossed paths with some of Quanah's boys. We lost some of the herd to them, but we found Digger. I reckon trading a few head of dumb cows for a good hand ain't too bad of a deal. Has there been any trouble around here?"

Forgotten Country　　　　　　　　　　　　　John Spiars

"There's been some fences cut and a few head of cattle have gone missing, but we ain't the only ones. Folks all along the river have been telling stories of night riders and missing cows. There's even been a few killings. I'd have talked to the law myself, but I didn't want to leave the place unwatched. That's why we're down to beans and corn pone. This bacon is the last of the meat, except for what's walking around the pasture, of course."

"You did the right thing, but we can't keep letting our cows go missing, and I hate a thief. After breakfast, I want you to put the boys to work. You can start by having 'em mend those fences, and I reckon I'll go have a talk with the sheriff."

"What's the sheriff gonna say? You know as well as I do that it's Mason Lorde's men who are behind the stealing."

"I know that," Heck said, sitting down to breakfast, "but we gotta give the law a chance to do their job. Lorde has three men to our one, so as long as I run this outfit, we'll be waiting a spell before we go to war with him."

With his second cup of coffee behind him, Heck walked to the barn and began to saddle his horse.

"I don't blame ya," Heck said, as the appaloosa bristled at the sight of a saddle. "I ain't overjoyed at the thought of a ten-mile ride either, but I reckon it's gotta be done."

After cinching up the girth, he gave her a good rub down with a curry comb. He figured it was the least he could do after pulling her away from her feed.

With a gentle nudge, horse and rider set off down the long drive. As he put the pasture land behind him, Heck passed through the peach and pear orchards, and after making his way across the Brazos River, he came to the main road that led straight into Weatherford. He had never imagined how a body could become attached to one place and never want to leave. To his mind, life had been an adventure and being tied down to one place was what a person did when they were too old and feeble to get out of the rocking chair. Now he saw that having a place of his own was what he wanted more than anything, and far from being a burden, it seemed to be the greatest adventure of all.

Chapter Fifteen

Parker County was the seat of wealth and power in North Texas and had been built almost entirely on the back of the hundred or so small ranches that covered the landscape. They had the numbers, and together, their cattle brought in most of the money that filled the local coffers, but there was only one man who wielded the real power in the county.

Mason Lorde's spread was twice as large as the next two largest ranches combined. He employed fifteen permanent hands, and twice that many during roundup and drives, though most were paid for their expertise with a gun instead of with cows. With his own army and a fortune to back him up, Mason Lorde had managed to bring most of the other ranches under his thumb. He promised to drive those who didn't do his bidding out of the territory, and

Heck figured the recent thefts represented just the opening salvo in a coming war.

Weatherford was the county seat for Parker County, and the wealth of the county was represented by the conspicuously ornate courthouse that loomed over downtown. It was made from pink limestone and rose to four stories, not including the clock tower, which was topped with a richly carved cupola. The portico was supported by five scalloped columns of alabaster marble, beneath which, the cattle barons conducted the real business of the county out of ear shot of the elected officials who were left to wait patiently for their marching orders.

As he trotted past the courthouse, Heck couldn't help but chuckle as he thought about how the politicians emerged on election day with chests puffed out, espousing all manner of promises, but they were, in reality, nothing more than puppets on a string.

Past the seat of local power and the row of fancy offices belonging to lawyers, business leaders, and bankers, was the Parker County Sheriff's office, which also housed the jail. It was a large two-story wooden structure that had been built by the founder of Weatherford as his personal residence. Somewhere along the way, the man had decided he deserved a bigger house, and the old one had been converted to the county jail.

The current sheriff was Lars Garhardt, and Heck thought him to be a good man, though it was widely known he was an old friend of Mason Lorde. The old timers in Parker County remembered that both men came to the area at the same time, but no one seemed to know where they had come from.

Forgotten Country   John Spiars

"Morning, Heck," Sheriff Garhardt said, from the comfort of a front porch rocking chair.

"Good morning, sheriff," Heck said, tying his horse to the hitching post.

"There's coffee on the stove, so help yourself."

"Thank ya, but I'm in town on business and then I gotta get back to the ranch. Ulley's done a good job with the place while I've been away, but I suspect there's been a lot left undone."

"Well, what brings ya to town?"

"To buy supplies, mainly. Hell, the boys will be fighting the cows for grass if we don't get the shelves stocked. But I also came here to talk to you. It seems we've had some fences cut and several head of cattle have come up missing."

Leaning back in the rocking chair, the sheriff scratched his graying beard and let out an exasperated sigh. "You came all the way out here to file a complaint for thievery? Dang, I figured a man like you would handle that sort of thing yourself."

"Ordinarily, I would," Heck said, "but I'm trying to avoid starting a range war."

"A range war?" the sheriff exclaimed, jumping to his feet. "We're just talking about some no-account cow thief."

"Sheriff, I think you know as good as I do that this ain't just one or two dregs stealing a couple of cows for whiskey money. Mason Lorde wants to force all the small ranchers out of the county and cutting fences and stealing stock is just the beginning. He'll keep upping the ante till we give up or we're six feet under."

"Keep your voice down," he whispered. Looking first left and then right, the sheriff assured himself that no one was within ear shot. "Someone could hear, and that really would start a war."

Opening the door, Sheriff Garhardt ushered Heck inside. He followed the lawman down a narrow hallway that led to the back of the office. After filling his coffee cup, Lars lowered his two-hundred and fifty pounds into a small chair at the kitchen table.

"Would you like me to draw the shades and check under the table for spies?" Heck said with feigned amusement.

"I ain't joking with ya, boy. Mason Lorde controls this county, ain't nothing can be done about that, but bucking him will lead to only misery. I told ya when you first come here that starting a ranch in Parker County was a bad idea and that you should sell and move elsewhere. I like you, Heck, and I don't want to see you get hurt, so I'm telling you the same thing now. Get out. Mason wants ya gone right now, and he'll give you a good price to sell, but if ya won't, he'll dig in and get mean."

"You're the law, so I'm asking ya to do your job."

"I gave ya good advice, Mister Carson, and that's the best service I can give you. Theft is a town matter, so if you want to swear out a complaint, you'll have to talk to the marshal in Ellsby."

"The Ellsby marshal is Otis Lorde, Mason's brother," Heck said.

"That's right, so just let the matter drop and get outta the territory. The cattle business is full of men just like Mason Lorde and you're better than their kind. The law is an honorable profession, and from what I've heard, you were a credit to your badge. Any town would be proud to have you as their marshal, and while you might not die rich, at least you'll put your head on your pillow each night with a clear conscience."

"Is your conscience clear, sheriff?"

"I'm a different story, son. I set my trail a long time ago, and it's too late for me, but it ain't for you."

"Thank ya for your time, sheriff. At least, now I know where I stand," Heck said, walking towards the door.

Walking in front of the dry goods store, Heck had just stepped onto the boardwalk, when he felt a hand grab his left arm. Reaching for his pistol, he spun around to face whatever new danger fate had thrown his way. Looking down, Heck saw the messenger boy from the telegraph office.

"Dang it, boy, that's a good way to get yourself shot. Don't ever grab a man like that."

"Sorry, Mister Carson, but I was trying to catch ya before ya went into the store," the boy said nervously. "I've got another telegraph from the governor. It was just luck that I saw ya on the street."

"It's okay, boy," Heck said, taking the message from him. "Just try to be careful."

As he read the paper, Heck couldn't believe his eyes. Reading it a second time, he hoped that his eyes had deceived him, but even after a third reading, the message didn't change.

Earl Mosby
Wanted for murder
Believed to be working for Mason Lorde

Cattle theft or not, the time for giving up and leaving had past. Earl Mosby was a gunman who had killed more than his share. He relished the reputation and fear that his killings inspired, but mostly he enjoyed working for Mason Lorde and being a big man in the county. If he was on Lorde's payroll, then the die was already cast, and a showdown with the cattle baron would be unavoidable.

Heck ordered his supplies, paid for them, and made arrangements for Darby to pick them up, after which, he mounted his horse and hit the trail for Ellsby. He figured that if a confrontation was coming, he would go ahead and shake the Lorde family tree a bit. Faced with a sworn warrant from the governor, Marshal Lorde would be forced to either turn over Mosby, or risk being removed from office, and Heck didn't much care which way thing's played out.

Chapter Sixteen

If the town of Weatherford was the showplace of the county, then Ellsby was its ugly, ne'er-do-well cousin. The buildings were mostly ramshackle structures made of clapboard or just about any other materials that could be used to create a dry spot out of the scorching sun.

At the moment, Heck wasn't in the market, but if he had been, he figured he could pick anyone off the streets of Ellsby and be assured of collecting a bounty. The main business in town was whiskey and women and they were available in every form imaginable. Saloons, gambling halls, houses of ill repute, and opium dens were tucked into every nook and corner, anywhere a few feet could be found, ill-gotten money was collected by the fist full. Such a town attracted the roughest sort, and in Ellsby, they roamed the streets, seemingly unafraid of any trouble from the law.

Mason Lorde would never dirty the soles of his boots by setting foot in Ellsby, but Heck recognized many of his men among the shiftless folk walking down the streets. They collected a portion of all the money made in town, and his brother, the marshal, kept just enough order so that the cash continued to flow. The only substantial structure in the whole forsaken place was the marshal's office and jail, where Marshal Otis Lorde could usually be found when he wasn't in one of the saloons or brothels. The jail cells rarely housed any real outlaws, mostly they were used for honest folk who failed to make their payments to Lorde or those who got in his way.

"I reckon being Mason Lorde's brother has its upside," Heck said to himself, as he stepped into the cavernlike darkness of the marshal's office. His sense of impending danger had him wary, and he removed the rawhide thong from around his pistol's hammer.

Two small windows cut into the top of the stone walls allowed in just enough light to add to the gloomy feel of the place. It put Heck in mind of the dungeons mentioned in the Bible, where early Christians were persecuted by the Romans, and he figured that decent people in Ellsby were just about as welcome as those Christians had been.

"Mister Carson," a voice called out from the darkness, "I was told to be expecting you."

Stepping into the dusty beams of light, Marshal Otis Lorde approached Heck, with an express gun pointed at his midsection.

"You must be a man with many enemies, Marshal," Heck said, slowly raising his hands, "or do you just not like visitors?"

"I like visitors just fine, as long as they're of my choosing. As far as enemies go, I'm tasked with upholding the law, so I have a whole town full of 'em. Which are you, Mister Carson, visitor or enemy?"

"Time will tell, but for now, I'm just a fellow lawman looking for a killer named Earl Mosby. I've got a paper on him from Governor Davis," Heck said, as he handed him the telegraph.

Marshal Lorde looked at the paper suspiciously, but satisfied he was in no immediate danger, he lowered his rifle.

"You're a brave man, Mister Carson. You've walked into the lion's den, but that don't mean you'll be able to walk out."

Lowering his arms, Heck said, "Marshal, you're a sworn man of the law, and you're holding a warrant from the governor himself. If you go against it, you'll lose your badge, and then what use will you be to your brother? I imagine having you in this office is worth more than one hired gun."

"Alright, Mister Carson. I can see you're a man who likes to take the bull by the horns, so I'll take ya to him. I expect we'll find him over at the Brazen Bull. The sporting women don't see customers till later in the day, so he should be downstairs in the saloon."

"Let's go pay him a visit then."

"Like I said, you sure like taking the bull by the horns," Marshal Lorde laughed, as he led the way out the door.

In the full light of the afternoon sun, Heck was able to get a good look at Marshal Lorde and was amused that the man's appearance matched the cavernous feel of his office.

Forgotten Country · John Spiars

His eyes were grayish-blue and bulged out of his head so that they seemed to balance on either side of his nose like a pair of Pince-Nez glasses. This, along with the grayish skin that hung on his bones like an ill-fitting suit of clothes, gave him the appearance of a lizard more than a man.

"When we get to the saloon, I'll back your play, but if bullets start flying, I'll be taking my leave. I don't intend to go to my grave, so you can collect some bounty," Lorde said, pointing toward the open door of the Brazen Bull.

"This town is certainly lucky to have you protecting their Christian virtues," Heck said, watching the motley rabble of Ellsby stumbling along the street, and wondering what kind of fork in the road had led them to this hell on earth.

"This is it, so go on in, and I'll watch your back from the door," the marshal said, yelling above the voices from inside the saloon.

"I feel better already," he said, pushing past the lawman.

Inside the dilapidated interior, a dozen men in various stages of unconsciousness, looked up through whiskey-soaked eyes as Heck entered the saloon.

The only ones who didn't seem to notice him was the saloon keeper and the three men who surrounded him. Two of the men held knives to the man's throat, while the other one appeared to be threatening him with a hatchet.

"You'd better hand the money over, cause my brother ain't drew blood all week and he's gettin' mighty anxious to color his blade. Ain't that right, Dev?" the man with the hatchet snarled.

"That's right, Cain, and it might as well be this fat sow here. I'd bleed him for a day before he took his last breath."

"Howdy, boys," Heck said, walking in their direction. He had only taken two steps when he felt a burning in the back of his skull, and the floor suddenly rushed up to meet him. He managed to get his arms out in front of him, which at least prevented him from busting his face on the wooden floor.

Shaking the cobwebs from his head, Heck watched as Otis Lorde snatched the Colt from his holster.

"You like taking the bull by the horns? Well, you got your hands full now," the marshal laughed, kicking Heck in the gut.

"Who's this, Otis?" Cain asked, shoving the saloon keeper to the floor.

"This here's Heck Carson, and he's a no-good bounty hunter who came to town looking for Earl. I thought you boys might like having a little fun with him, but ya can't kill him. I reckon my brother will want to be having words with him first."

"Sure," Cain said. "That sounds like more fun than cuttin' this whiskey peddler to ribbons. Devlin, Zeke, let's kill a little time beating this fella, at least till the workin' girls are ready for business."

Standing over Heck, with his rifle cradled in his arms, Marshal Lorde pushed Heck over with the tip of his boot.

"Heck, I'd like ya to meet some friends of mine. These are the Slater brothers, Cain, Devlin and Zeke. They work for my brother, Mason. We've got what ya might call a family business."

Looking up at the three men, it wasn't hard to tell they were related. It appeared the three hadn't seen soap and water in quite some time, and their tattered clothes were even more filthy than the men wearing them. As the brothers smiled, Heck was sure the sum total of their teeth couldn't have been more than five.

Cain walked over to Heck, and he saw that the man wore two hatchets held in place by a rope wrapped around his soiled overalls. They weren't exactly practical weapons against a rifle or pistol, but Heck was sure he didn't want to be on the business end of them. Without saying a word, he lifted a leg and prepared to deliver a kick to Heck's face, but seeing it coming, Heck blocked the man's boot with his arms, and then in one motion he lifted and twisted it, throwing the man to the ground.

Jumping to his feet, Heck picked up a chair and brought it down on Devlin's head as the man charged him. Zeke Slater threw a wild punch aimed at his head, and though he was certainly no pugilist, had his fist connected with Heck's head, the fight would surely have been over.

Heck ducked the punch and delivered a right and left jab to the big man's nose, breaking it with a sickening crunch.

After making it to his feet, Cain lunged for Heck, but was sent flying backwards by a knee to his head. He landed on a table, which shattered to splinters under his weight.

"You boys sure are a disappointment," Otis Lorde said, shaking his head. "I reckon I'll have to lend ya a hand."

Grabbing his rifle by the barrel, the marshal swung it like a club, and brought the stock down across Heck's back. Heck dropped to his knees, as the throbbing in his head was replaced by the one in his back. He attempted to make it to his feet, but was knocked back down by another blow, this one landing on his right shoulder.

"There ya go, boys," Marshal Lorde said. "Ya think y'all can take him now?"

Never ones to quibble over things like fairness, the Slaters seized their chance for revenge. The three delivered multiple kicks and punches to Heck's head, stomach and back, delighting in the damage they were inflicting on him. Under the beating he was receiving, it was useless for Heck to try and stand, so he did his best to cover his head and to try and prevent any permanent damage.

After a few minutes of being kicked and punched, Heck was almost unconscious and unable to put up any kind of defense. The Slaters soon became bored and tired from the beating and decided to have a different kind of fun. They drew their blades and prepared to carve Heck up, cackling wildly as they thought of the fun they would have slicing into the famous Texas Ranger.

"Hold it right there, boys," the marshal said. "I told ya, we need to keep him alive."

"I'm gonna chop this fella into cord wood," Cain said, raising his hatchet.

"Later," Lorde said, "but for now, we gotta get him over to the jail. My back's plumb give out, so you boys will have to take him."

"Dang it, Otis, you sure know how to spoil a man's fun," Cain said, finally stepping away from Heck and sheathing his hatchet. "Alright, boys, y'all grab a hold of him and get him over to the jail. We'll have some more fun with this fella after Mister Lorde is done with him."

Picking Heck up by the arms, the brothers lifted his battered and bloodied body off the ground and dragged him from the Brazen Bull.

CHAPTER SEVENTEEN

Heck woke up on a thin mattress which offered little protection from the metal bed frame underneath. It felt as though it were filled with mesquite thorns and brambles that stuck him in the back, though the pain in his ribs hurt much worse. With each breath, the stabbing pain in his side made him wince, and as the numbness wore off, the throbbing made his head feel as though it were in a vice. His blackened eyes were swollen so that he was forced to look around through thin slits, which combined with the ringing in his head, gave him a blurry image of his surroundings.

The room was no more than seven feet square and was built from blocks of limestone, which without the benefit of a window, was even more gloomy than the office. Slowly, his eyes grew accustomed to the darkness, and he made out the form of a man standing in the corner. Trying to see past the blurry haze that had settled over his head, Heck saw that the figure was a man, and judging from the fancy clothes he was wearing, he was not a fellow prisoner.

"Who are you?" Heck asked. The pain in his ribs made him grit his teeth with each word.

"I'm Doctor Grant, and though I served the Union in the late war, I am no relation. I am currently in the service of Mason Lorde as town doctor, and the good marshal wanted me to be sure you didn't expire prematurely. When I first saw you, I thought that might be a possibility, but once I cleaned the blood off, I was satisfied that your injuries were not terminal."

Like so many doctors who practiced medicine along the frontier, Doctor Grant was apparently a drunk, and he slurred so badly that Heck had to think about the man's words for a moment in order to figure out what he was trying to say.

"I'm glad to hear that, Doc, but I don't reckon it makes much difference, cause I don't imagine they plan on keeping me around too long anyhow."

The doctor looked at his feet and then at the ceiling, trying to think of a polite way to answer. A drunk or not, Heck appreciated the man's effort, though it was hardly necessary. Heck was not one to shy away from things, especially the truth.

"Knowing Mason Lorde and his brother, that's probably true, but as long as you're in my care, I'll do whatever I can for you. What did you do to earn such treatment from these ruffians?"

Heck sat up on the bed so as to get a better look at the man he was talking to, but as he did, the pain from his ribs and the swimming in his head caused him to double over and almost fall off the edge of the bed.

"My name's Heck Carson, and I came to town to take Earl Mosby into custody, but it appears I misjudged the marshal. I figured he'd be forced to obey an order from the governor, but it would seem he has no regard for the law, and he's also dumber than a box of rocks."

"That's our marshal, alright," the doctor said with a slight chuckle, "but it makes sense they wouldn't be so eager to give up Earl Mosby. He's certainly kept me busy with patients, but he's provided even more work for the undertaker. His skills seem to be the most in demand around here these days."

"Yeah, I've crossed paths with him once or twice in Weatherford, but I never had paper on him, so we were never formerly introduced."

"It's just as well. Most of those that meet his acquaintance are laid out in front of the undertaker soon after. Come to think of it, though, if you're the Heck Carson I've heard so much about, they say the same about you."

"Well, those are mostly just stories, Doc. I ain't killed nobody in several weeks," Heck said, managing a painful smile.

The two men talked casually for over an hour, covering both their experiences during the war, and laughing at the absurdity of two people who had traveled such different paths, winding up in the same no-account town and at the mercy of the same crooked cattle baron. Doc Grant was a highly educated man given to the use of big words whose meaning Heck could only guess at, but he liked the doctor and appreciated the fact that he took the time to talk with him. Heck had done the same for others in his position, condemned men who soon had a date with the gallows. He had never been sure that he ever made much of a difference, but it seemed to him that if a man was of a mind to talk, then he should have someone to listen in his final hours.

Their conversation was cut short by the sound of a key turning in the lock, followed by Marshal Lorde stepping through the door.

"Mister Carson," the marshal said, almost spitting the words, "it seems you've been granted a reprieve. Doc Grant, your services are no longer needed here, but the barkeep from the Brazen Bull is over at your office, and he could do with some help."

Heck stood up but had to balance himself on the wall to keep from falling. Taking a deep breath and steading himself, he carefully put one foot in front of the other, and made it to the door, where he was forced to grab the frame for support.

"Ya sure you know what you're doing, Doc? This feller looks like he's on death's door," Marshal Lorde said, fairly pleased with himself for Heck's condition.

"He'll be just fine, as long as he rests and doesn't suffer any further damage."

"I can't promise ya any of that, but as long as he leaves my jail on his own, I've upheld my duty," the marshal said, leading the men back to the outer office.

His eyes seemed to be swollen worse than before, and Heck had to force them open enough to see a few feet in front of him. Light streamed in through the small windows, causing him to close his eyes tightly and shield them with his arm. Doctor Grant took hold of his right arm and led him to the marshal's desk, where he was given his guns and knife.

"Where's my horse, marshal?" Heck asked. His senses were clearing enough that he was growing angry at the marshal's part in his misery, and for being a disgrace to his badge.

"Your horse is over at the livery, and you can pay the stable boy when you pick it up. You've got yourself a fine appaloosa there. I was just about to claim her for myself."

"Sorry to disappoint ya, marshal, but I reckon we can settle up the next time we meet," Heck said, as he opened the door and stepped outside.

The sun was low in the sky, but just at the right height to shine in Heck's eyes and cause his head to throb more than it already did. He was about to ask directions to the livery, when he saw his horse in front of him, being held in place by Digger. Next to him sat Darby, Jefferson and Sheriff Garhardt.

The doctor helped Heck to his horse. "Can I be of any further assistance, Mister Carson?"

"Thanks, Doc, but it looks like I've got my own escort. What do I owe ya for the doctoring?"

"You don't owe me anything, Mister Carson. Just promise me you'll try to stay alive long enough to settle with those responsible. This ain't much of a town, but the folks here deserve better than Mason Lorde and his hired killers."

"I'll do what I can," Heck said, shaking the doctor's hand. "There'll be a reckoning, that's for sure."

"Dang, Heck," Darby said, looking at his friend and employer, "them boys sure laid in to you good."

"That's true enough, but what are you fellas doing here?"

"When ya didn't come back, we went to Weatherford looking for ya. The sheriff said you were headed here and we figured you had run into trouble."

"That's right," Sheriff Garhardt interrupted. "I ran into the boy from the telegraph office and he told me about the message from the governor, so I sent a message back to him asking for his help. He ordered me to help you bring in Earl Mosby, and he also gave me authority to take custody of you. Marshal Lorde had no choice but to release you to me once I showed him the order from Governor Davis."

Jefferson looked at his brother and his anger boiled even more than Heck's. "You want us to help you burn this worthless town to the ground, Heck? We can start with the jail and that no good marshal."

"We ain't doing no such thing, Jeff," Heck said, happy to see that his usually mild brother was able to work up such anger on his behalf. "We'll go with the sheriff here and take Earl Mosby into custody, which should light a spark in Mason Lorde and his brother the marshal. They'll end up making a play, and then we can come down on 'em like a hammer, and we'll be within the limits of the law when we do."

Heck put his feet in the stirrup and took a shallow breath to stifle the pain from his ribs, which seared through his body like a red-hot poker.

As his horse ambled along, Heck's body shook with each step and he swore he could feel every bruise and cut. Only when they reached the open range, where the horses could gallop, and he could get into rhythm with its gate, did the pain finally subside to a more manageable level.

Chapter Eighteen

Mason Lorde's ranch stretched over two-thousand acres of the lushest pasture land in the county and was situated along the widest part of the Brazos, where it turned southward. The placement not only insured him plenty of water for his cows, but also provided a tidy income by allowing him to dam the river and charge the ranchers downstream for water.

Heck, Darby, and Sheriff Garhardt rode up the path to Lorde's massive house, while Digger and Jefferson positioned themselves on a height, which looked down on the main house as well as the bunkhouse. The two were ordered to cover both building with their rifles, though the task was made difficult by the fact that the sun had disappeared from view, replaced by almost total darkness. The sheriff believed the best approach was to ride straight in and show Mason Lorde the warrant for Earl Mosby, but since there was no guarantee of success, having a couple of rifles covering them couldn't hurt.

Mason Lorde's home was built from milled lumber in a decidedly northern style, and its size and opulence created the perfect setting for Lorde to survey his vast kingdom. The whole spread was a testament to excess and show over practicality, which was a trait of those born to money that Heck could never understand.

"When we get to the house, I want you to let me do all of the talking," Sheriff Garhardt said. "This could go bad really quick and the three of us would be caught in the crossfire. I don't know about you boys, but I don't intend to have my life cut short because you want to start a raucous over some missing cows and a beating."

"I've got no problem with that, sheriff," Heck said. "I just want to collect my reward on this fella and then find a place where I don't have to move for at least a week."

After stopping in front of the house, Sheriff Garhardt dismounted, while Heck and Darby stayed on their horses. Heck cradled his Greener in his arms and Darby pulled his Remington, which he concealed in his lap for easy access.

"Lars? What are you doing here at this hour?" Mason Lorde asked, surprised to see his old friend at his door. "Who are these men you've brought with you?"

"I'm here on official business, Mason. I have a warrant, sworn out by the governor himself, for the arrest of Earl Mosby."

"That all sounds very serious, Lars, but are you sure you want to push this? Austin is a long way from here, and you're all alone. You could just forget this whole matter."

"I can't do that, Mason. One of the men with me is a bounty hunter named Heck Carson, and he's got a real bur in his saddle about doing his duty. Even if I let this thing go, he's not about to."

The cattle baron rubbed his temples and let out an exasperated breath before stepping onto the porch and closing the door behind him.

"Ah, yes. Several of my boys had a disagreement with Mister Carson, I believe. Isn't that right, Cain?"

"It sure is, Mister Lorde, but me and my brothers made quick work of him," Cain Slater yelled, as he walked from the bunkhouse to the main house. He was followed closely by his brothers, Zeke and Devlin.

"I can see that," Mason Lorde said, straining to look at Heck by the light of the torches that illuminated the front of his home. "That man should be under the care of a doctor. He looks like he's been trampled by a herd of buffalo."

"You want me to finish him, Mister Lorde?" Cain said, strumming his finger on the butt of his pistol. "I can blow him out of the saddle right now."

"I encourage you to try," Heck said, "but you and your brothers will be dead before you clear your holster."

"He can't kill us all," a man said, emerging from the bunkhouse. "They say Carson is fast, but I'm faster."

Heck recognized Earl Mosby instantly, but even if he hadn't, Heck would have pegged him as a gun hand right off. He wore stove pipe boots made of soft leather, a silk shirt, and an expensive vest with a paisley design, certainly not the dress of a cowboy. The ivory handled Colt that rode high on his hip was nickel plated and cost more than the average ranch hand made in a year. More than the man's dress, it was the way he carried himself that gave away his profession. He had an air of confidence and a swagger, born of an absolute certainty in his ability to defeat his enemies, no matter who they might be.

"You're Earl Mosby," Heck said, tipping his hat. "I have a warrant for your arrest, and I'd be obliged if you'd come along without any trouble."

"That's not likely to happen, friend," Mosby said, stepping a few feet from where Heck sat. He let his hands fall to his side and spread his legs slightly. "You do see we've got the numbers to send all of you to hell."

Through the corner of his eye, Heck watched Mosby, but he spoke to Mason Lorde. "Mister Lorde, Mosby is just one man, but if you push this, you'll lose a lot more. We've got two men with rifles on that rise, and they'll open up on the whole bunch of ya if there's any trouble."

"He's lying, Mister Lorde," Cain Slater said. "We beat him once and we can do it again."

"Don't be a fool, Mason," Sheriff Garhardt said. "Nobody has to die here tonight. I'm your friend and I really don't want to shoot you, but I've chosen a side and there ain't no retreating from it now."

"Listen to me," Mason Lorde said. "Any man that draws his gun can find himself another job. We're not gonna start a war over one man. Earl, the law is the law, and you're gonna have to answer for any crimes you've committed."

"But Mister Lorde, they're liable to hang me. You're just gonna let 'em take me?" he asked, almost pleading.

"I'm sorry, Mosby, but I'm a law-abiding man, and I believe everyone has to answer for what they've done. You believe that too, don't you Lars? Like you said, you've chosen a side."

"That's a fact," Sheriff Garhardt said, walking over to Earl Mosby. "Get this man a horse so we can take him out of here."

"Don't forget what I said," Mason yelled, all humor gone from his tone. "We all must answer for what we've done, even old friends like you, Lars."

Earl Mosby's horse was quickly brought out and Sheriff Garhardt helped him into the saddle, after taking his gun and searching him for any other weapons. "I'm sure you're angry, Mason, but I'd ask that you think things over clearly before you act. You may be the power in these parts, but I'm the duly elected law, and that still means something."

"That badge won't stop what you've got coming, Lars. I've things to settle with Mister Carson here, but I hate a traitor above all else. Keep thinking about that until we see each other again."

After securing their prisoner, the group began the tiring trek back to Weatherford, but none of them had the sense that their fight was over.

"You realize that your friend is now your enemy, don't ya, sheriff?" Heck said, riding next to Lars Garhardt.

"He made that pretty clear back there at the ranch. I've known Mason Lorde longer than anybody. He's a man to carry a grudge to the grave, and no one knows that better than me."

"Then why did ya choose to help us? You could have lined up with your friend and just gone on living the good life."

Sheriff Garhardt stared into the darkness for a long moment before answering. "That warrant for Mosby says he murdered an old man and his wife. He set their home on fire with them in it and let them burn to death. If I'm going to call myself a lawman, there's no way I could let him go, and I couldn't side with a man that would pay him to do something like that. Mason and I have travelled many miles together, but not so many that I could ever be alright with something like that."

"Do ya figure you'll be able to hold me?" Earl Mosby said, with a grin that was visible, even in the darkness.

"You'll stand trial, and afterwards, I'll be walking you up the steps of the gallows, don't ya be worrying about that."

"We'll see, sheriff. We'll surely see about that."

Chapter Nineteen

A week of bed rest helped to heal Heck's wounds so that he could once again climb into the saddle, though it took another week before he could ride around his ranch without severe pain.

"Are we gonna finally get some real work out of you today?" Jefferson asked, over their breakfast of biscuits and bacon. "When I agreed to help you out up here, I didn't know I'd be doing all of your work. The Santa Gertrudis are mixing well with those broken-down bovines of yours, and with any luck, by this time next year, we'll have a pasture full of cows. But for any of that to happen, much work will be required."

"You don't have to worry about me, brother. I'm back on my feet and ready to devote all of my energies to the ranch. With the reward money for Earl Mosby, we're flush with cash to boot."

"I'm glad to hear it," Jefferson said, "but if you're serious, you might consider naming this place. It would at least finally seem more like home, and it's easier for men to ride for the brand when there is one."

"I've been telling him that all along," Ulley said, placing a biscuit stuffed with bacon in his mouth.

"You say a lot of things, Ulley," Heck said, standing up, "but most of it I just choose to ignore."

"And that is your problem, boss," Ulley replied. "Ya hired me, but you don't listen to a word I say. You get your brother to come here and help, but ya don't listen to him either. It don't make any sense."

"Heck knows what he's doing," Digger said, rushing to his friend's defense. "You should've seen how he fought off those Comanche. He can do anything, and he'll make this place go too. You just watch."

"Thanks, kid. You held your own against those Indians, too, and we'll make a cowboy out of you as well, but I reckon we'd both be better off if we listened to Ulley and Jeff. They're real cowboys, and as much as it pains me to say so, they know what they're talking about."

"In that case, I suggest we all quit loafing and get some work done," Jefferson said, walking to the door.

"Darby must be getting hungry, so I'll go relieve him on patrol," Heck said. "We must have made Lorde mighty mad by taking one of his best guns off his own ranch. I figure he'll be making his next play before long."

"You say that like it's a good thing," Ulley said.

"I don't know how we're supposed to run a ranch and prepare for next year's drive if we're busy shootin' it out with Lorde's killers, or if we're all dead."

"This place won't never amount to anything as long as Mason Lorde and the other cattle barons are set on running us out, so yes, if a war's gotta come, it's better that it comes now. Digger, you can relieve me in a few hours."

As he walked from the house to the barn, Heck could see a rider coming up the drive at a gallop. It took only a few seconds for him to get close enough for Heck to recognize him. It was the message boy from the telegraph office in Weatherford.

Taking the telegraph from the boy, Heck figured it must be another job from the governor, and he was prepared to send a message back declining the job. However, after reading it, his jaw tightened in anger, and he dismissed the boy without his usual gratuity.

With the piece of paper gripped tightly between his fingers, he walked into the house and began putting supplies in his saddle bag.

"You're taking four boxes of ammunition just to ride fences?" Jefferson said. "Has the war started already?"

"It would appear so," Heck replied, handing his brother the telegraph.

Caroline Farber taken by two men
Marshal is away
Recommend you come at once

Grabbing his Henry from the gun rack next to the fireplace, Heck placed it on the table.

"What do ya plan on doing, brother, go after her by yourself? You'll get you and her both killed."

"Don't be a danged fool," Ulley said. "You've got work to do, and if it's a war ya want, you've got one brewing right here. Traipsing off to Uvalde don't make no sense."

"I'm gonna take the train from Fort Worth and with any luck, I'll be back in a week. Surely you can hold things together that long."

"Of course, I can, but your brother's right, you can't go by yourself. I'll manage on my own," Ulley said, giving in to Heck despite his earlier protest.

"I don't plan on going by myself, that would serve no good purpose. I'll be taking Jefferson and Digger with me."

"No," Ulley replied. "You should take Darby too. Next to you, he's the best gun we got."

"Like ya said, troubles coming with Mason Lorde, so I'm gonna leave Darby here to help ya and I don't want no argument about it."

"You mean I get to go with ya on the train," Digger said excitedly.

"That's right, kid. Go pack some supplies for yourself, and don't forget to wear the pistol I gave ya. We'll all want to take rifles as well, and Ulley, please get us some dried meat, beans and coffee for the trip."

"You're the boss, Heck," Ulley said.

Pulling down his rifle, Jefferson lowered his voice to a whisper and said, "Wouldn't it be better to take Darby and leave the boy here to help Ulley? Like he said, next to you, Darby's the best gun we got, and you ain't fully healed yet."

"I'm leaving him here because he's a good gun. Ulley will need someone that's good in a fight to watch his backside. Digger, saddle your horse and find Darby. Tell him to come back here double quick."

"I suppose it's occurred to you this might be a trap?"

"I've got more than my share of enemies out there, so I don't answer the call of nature without checking over my shoulder, but that can't stop me from doing what's gotta be done."

Pulling his Greener from the rack, he handed it to Jefferson, and then reached in the top drawer of the bureau beneath the gun rack, and grabbed his Derringer, placing it in his vest pocket.

"I hope it doesn't come to us depending on that for our survival," Jefferson said, eyeing the Derringer.

"It's saved my life more than once. Now, let's saddle up and get on our way."

The train depot in Fort Worth was the newest building in town, as well as the busiest. Located south of the stockyards, the Spanish-style structure was crowded with ranchers and other businessmen, flush with cash and each one in a big hurry to get somewhere.

"Golly, Heck," Digger said, as he stared in amazement at the mass of humanity rushing along the various platforms. "Where are all these folks headed?"

"Their business is none of our affair. Keep your mind set on your own doings, otherwise, you're apt to have your head in the clouds when you need to be thinking clearly," Heck said, locating the train bound for San Antonio.

"That's good advice, brother," Jefferson said. "I wish you'd take it yourself. You say you want to be a rancher, but you won't lay down your gun long enough to put in the work."

"That's our train there," Heck said, pointing to the platform on the far side of the depot.

Taking their places on the wooden bench, the three sat in silence as the train steamed south. Digger looked out the window, watching in awe as the countryside sped by. As Heck looked at the wonder in his eyes, he was reminded that Digger was but a boy, and suddenly regretted his decision to bring him along. Heck had always believed that regret was a waste of time, but in the silent rhythm of the swaying train, he wondered if he had rescued Digger only for him to be killed at the hands of his enemies.

"It would seem some of my words took hold after all," Jefferson said, sensing the regret that Heck was feeling. Despite himself, he viewed this with some satisfaction.

"What would you have me do, just let Caroline be sacrificed because of me?"

"You don't know that this has anything to do with you. Uvalde is a dangerous place, especially for a woman. She could have been taken by Comancheros, slavers from south of the border, or just some no-account outlaws looking for a woman."

"That don't make me feel any better," Heck said. "She needs my help and I'm gonna do whatever I can for her."

"That's it, ain't it? You'd rather try and save the world than work on building a life of your own. The thing you'd better ask yourself is how many people are gonna be sacrificed to your quest?"

Heck closed his eyes and leaned back in his seat. "You can back out any time you want, brother. The only question I have is, can I count on you or not?"

"I'm with ya all the way," Jefferson said, "but unlike the boy here, I'm your brother, and it's my place to die beside you."

Forgotten Country   John Spiars

It was well after dark by the time their train steamed into San Antonio, and after retrieving their horses and gear, they secured a room at the first hotel they came to. The three were exhausted, but they were even more hungry, so after convincing the owner to open the kitchen, they sat down to frijoles, tortillas, and a bit of cold beef.

"That might be the tastiest meal I've ever sat down to," Jefferson said, stuffing his mouth with the last tortilla.

"Your first meal after going a spell without food always taste's good," Heck replied. "I've had that experience quite a few times over the years."

"I reckon that's another good thing about ranch life, you ain't gotta miss too many meals."

Filling his cup from a pitcher of water, Heck stared at a spot on the wall, momentarily lost in thought.

"I've seen the sun set over the Rocky Mountains and rise over the Atlantic Ocean. I've ridden into country that has scarcely been seen by anyone other than Indians, and I've witnessed acts of such selfless bravery that you wouldn't believe me if I told you. If missing a few meals is the price I had to pay for all of that, then it was well worth it. Along the way, I've also loved and lost two women, but I don't intend to lose Caroline Farber. Building the ranch won't mean nothing without someone to share it with, so when I get her back, I plan on making her my wife."

"When did ya decide on that?" Jefferson asked, shocked by his brother's sudden desire at matrimony.

"I reckon I've known it for quite some time, but it came to me just now."

"Well then," Jefferson said, rising from his chair. "Let's get some shut eye so we can get your woman back, hopefully without getting ourselves killed doing it."

Retiring to their room, the three drew straws to determine which two would get the bed and who would sleep on the floor.

Never one to linger over his losses, Heck spread his bed roll on the wooden floor and prepared for an uncomfortable night's sleep. As he began to drift off, he was pulled back from sleep by Digger's voice.

"Heck, you still awake?"

"Yeah, kid. I'm awake," Heck yawned.

"Did you really see all that, you know, what you was telling Jefferson about?"

"I saw all that and a lot more besides."

"You've had quite a life, Heck."

"It's just a life, the same as any other. It's been some good, some bad, and a whole bunch of just putting one foot in front of the other. I reckon yours will be pretty much the same."

"I wanna see all I can. I don't want to be like my ma and pa. They worked their whole lives and then it was all over, without meaning a thing."

"That ain't true, kid. They left you behind, so as long as you make your life count, then theirs does too. Now, I've gotta sleep on this hard floor, so let me get to it."

Chapter Twenty

Two days in the saddle, with little sleep, brought Heck, Jefferson and Digger within the town limits of Uvalde. The midday sun made certain that those who were able, stayed indoors, so there were very few people on the street.

Heck didn't know what to expect, but if they were riding into a trap, he wanted to be prepared. He trusted his brother, but Jefferson was not accustomed to having enemies, so he hadn't developed the habit of watching all directions at once for signs of trouble. It would be up to Heck to see the trouble before it happened and to warn the others. He knew Jefferson could handle himself in a fight, but he wasn't sure how Digger would react, so Heck figured he'd have to save himself and the boy if things went wrong.

Forgotten Country   John Spiars

    The quietness of the town left Heck feeling wary and more than once he checked his pistol to make sure it set loose in its holster. His eyes moved continuously from left to right, while also looking up to check the roofs and balconies of the buildings. The few people who braved the heat on the boardwalk didn't seem to pay the strangers any heed, but as Heck knew, that didn't mean their presence had gone unnoticed.

    Reining their horses to a stop in front of the hotel, the three dismounted and walked inside. Standing at the front desk was a familiar face that immediately put Heck at ease.

    "Señor Heck, it is good to see you," Ernesto said, stepping from behind the desk to greet his friend.

    "This is my brother, Jefferson, and the boy is named Digger."

    "It is an honor to meet you both," Ernesto said warmly. "Señor Heck is a hero to this town and a welcomed guest in my hotel. I don't know if he told you, but he once saved the people of Uvalde from some very bad men."

    "That don't surprise me none," Digger said proudly. "Heck's the bravest man around."

    "Yes, one day they'll build statues in his honor and his legend will live on in songs," Jefferson said, looking at Heck to be sure he caught the mocking tone of his comment.

    Heck chose to ignore his brother's comment and got down to the business they had come to Uvalde for. "Ernesto, we're here to find Miss Farber. Please tell us what happened."

    "I knew you would come for her, Señor Heck. Others said you would not, but I knew you would. It would be best if you follow me. There are others who know much more than me."

Heck and the others followed Ernesto into the dining room, where several men were seated around a table.

"Good afternoon, Mister Carson. It certainly took you long enough to get here." The greeting came from an older man, dressed in a light-colored suit with a tan bowler hat. He had a slight paunch around the mid-section, and the thick spectacles he wore made him appear somewhat older than he probably was.

"Doc White? You mean they ain't run you outta town for killing one of your patients yet?" Heck said, shaking the mans had vigorously.

"He ain't done nothing yet that the law can prove," one of the men seated with the doctor said. He wore the silver star of a deputy marshal, but somehow the badge didn't seem to fit the man.

"Howdy, Hank. When did they make you marshal?" Heck asked. "I figured you'd be one on the other side of a jail cell."

"That's true enough, but I ain't the marshal. I'm just minding the store while the marshal's gone. They pinned this badge on me when Miss Farber was taken," Hank said, taking a serious tone. "We weren't sure what would happen next, but so far there ain't been no other trouble. I've organized a couple of search parties, but none of us are trackers, so we haven't seen any sign of her or the ones that took her."

"That's why I sent you the telegraph, Heck," Doc White said. "I knew you'd be the one to find her."

"I told them not to bother," the third man at the table said. "The men that took her did it for money, and as soon as they make their demand, I'll pay it."

Heck had noticed Horace Snow, but as had become his nature, he never wasted his time with fools.

"You think money solves everything, don't you, Horace? Why don't ya have those two idgets that fight your battles go out and find her?"

"They are no longer in my employ. One day, Heck, you'll learn that money does solve everything. Caroline is my woman, and I want you to stay out of this, or I'll put my money to work against you."

Reaching across the table, Heck grabbed Horace by his shirt with one hand and pulled him across the table.

"The last time I was in town, I chose to leave without settling with you, mainly because you're a fool, but if you get in my way, I will end you without losing a minute's sleep over it. Do we understand each other?"

As Heck held him by the collar, Horace could do nothing but nod his head.

"Take it easy, son," Doc White said, putting his hand on the younger man's shoulder. "Caroline wanted nothing to do with him after she learned that he sent those men after you."

Pulling Horace to his feet, Heck shoved him towards the door. "Get out of here before I give in to my less Christian side." Returning to the table, Heck sat down and said, "Tell me what happened, Doc."

"Two men rode into town and snatched her right off the street and then just as quickly, they rode out again. Nobody got a good look at the riders, or their horses either. Like we said, the marshal was out of town, so Hank organized some men and went looking for her, but they never found anything."

"Hank, do you know which way they were going when they left town?" Heck asked.

"To the west, I believe, but that's just what I was told. I wasn't on the street when it happened."

"You say you organized a group of men? Was Horace with ya?" Heck asked.

"Horace? He'd have been too worried about getting them fancy suits dirty."

The seed of an idea was beginning to take root in Heck's mind, but he didn't like the way things were shaping up.

"Did Horace go out and look on his own?"

"I never saw him. How about you, Doc?" Hank asked, turning to Doctor White.

"No, I don't recall that he ever lifted a finger to do anything. He stays in town all day, except for the times he rides out to look in on his family's spread. It's been deserted since his mother passed, but he's been working to fix it up for sale."

"He's been working on it by himself?"

"As far as I know, it's been just him."

"He don't strike me as being very handy," Heck said, trying to make sense of everything that he had learned. Turning to Digger and Jefferson he said, "Let's ride out west and see what we can find."

"It'll be dark soon," Jefferson said. "Hadn't we best wait till morning?"

"The early bird gets the worm, Jeff."

"I'm coming with ya, Heck," Hank said.

"No, it'd be best if you stayed here in town. You're the only law around, and there could still be trouble," Heck said.

"Let's get to it, boys," Jefferson said. "Times wasting."

Before leaving, Heck took Hank aside and said, "Keep an eye on Horace. I don't know what his play is, but I promise ya, it ain't good."

"I'll do it, Heck, but if ya know something, you need to go ahead and tell me."

"I don't know anything for sure yet, but when I do, you'll be the first to know."

Chapter Twenty-One

Following the road west out of town, Heck, Jefferson and Digger moved slowly, trying to find some sign that the others had missed.

"We've travelled at least five miles down this road and I ain't seen so much as a jack rabbit track," Heck said, checking the horizon through his field glass.

"I don't think they would have come this far," Jefferson said. "I've driven herds through here many times, and the country west of here is pretty desolate. It's just a whole lot of nothing."

Putting his field glass away, Heck wiped his brow, contemplating his next move. "They could have taken that cutoff we passed about a mile back, but that just leads up into the hills. The terrain is nothing but rock and there ain't

Forgotten Country   John Spiars

nothing living up there but lizards, rattlesnakes and maybe a mountain lion or two."

"Like I said before, none of this makes any sense," Jefferson said, turning his horse around and falling in behind Heck.

After a mile, they came to a narrow path that veered off to the south, cutting through a field of tall, wispy grass that was too dry even for cows to feed on. The path led to the top of a hill at such a steep slant that the horses quickly had to lower their head in order to pull themselves and their riders up it.

The grasslands soon gave way to dry earth and rocks, where each step became a perilous decision for the animals, lest they slip and break a leg, or plummet to their deaths. There was nothing along either side of the trail except for sheer rocky cliffs which dropped off into overgrown crevasses where even the scrubby mesquite trees had to struggle for survival. At the top of the rocky peak the trail split. One direction led further into the hills, while the other turned back to the east.

As he peered through his field glass, Jefferson looked over the vast desolation of the high country, which was imposing in its ruggedness, but also beautiful in a strong, noble way. It gave one the sense of looking on a wild animal, which was at once deadly and vulnerable.

"What do ya think?" Jefferson asked. "They would have had to keep moving south, right? The other direction would lead them back towards town."

"That's exactly what they did brother," Heck said, with the confidence of a man who had figured out a mystery but was troubled by the answer he had found.

"This was all part of his plan to mislead us. We must get back to Uvalde as quickly as we can."

Taking the trail to the east, they made good time down the other side of the hill, though the going was still quite treacherous. At the bottom of the hill, the game trail snaked just south of town, but a cutoff led them straight back to Uvalde in half the time it would have taken using the main road.

Heck and his companions made it through town without being noticed, and under the cover of darkness, they tied their horses in the alley behind the marshal's office. After pounding on the back door, it was finally opened by Hank, who greeted the nighttime visitors with a pistol in each hand.

"Dang boys, y'all are lucky I didn't just start shooting without looking to see who it was. I ain't grown comfortable with the weight of this badge, in fact, I'll be mighty happy when the marshal gets back to town."

"Well, I hate to bring ya bad news, but unless I'm wrong, the marshal ain't coming back."

"What do ya mean he ain't coming back?" Hank stammered.

"One way or another, he was removed so there'd be no one to make a legal fuss over Miss Farber. What has Horace been up to?"

Hank pulled out three metal cups from a shelf and poured a cup of coffee for the three of them. "After taking his supper at the café, Horace paid a visit to the bank, and then retired to his house. The lights went out about an hour ago, so I don't reckon we'll see him till morning. I've got a deputy watching his house just in case."

"I figure him to make his move early, so we'd all better be ready. I'd like for your deputy to come with us when we follow Horace out of town."

"You mean you think Horace Snow is involved in all of this?" Hank asked, though without much surprise.

"That's about the size of it, I'm afraid," Heck said, taking a sip from his coffee cup.

Digger looked at the thick, black mud in his own cup, unsure if he was meant to drink it or chew it.

"Something wrong with your coffee, boy?" Hank asked.

His question drew grins from both Heck and Jefferson but seemed to embarrass the young man.

"I ain't never had coffee before, that's all."

"Well, it's a good time to start, and I make the best coffee in town. It'll fortify ya against the cold, the travails of life, and even hell itself."

"Drink it and then go lay down in one of those bunks over yonder," Heck said, his voice taking on a fatherly tone that he hardly recognized as his own. "I don't know what we'll be facing tomorrow, but a man handles himself better if he's had sleep." Taking his own advice, Heck leaned back in his chair and covered his eyes with his hat.

A few hours before sunrise, Heck awoke to the sound of the front door creaking on its hinges. With a smooth motion that would have gone unnoticed by all but the most experienced gun hands, he drew his peacemaker and pulled back the hammer. With it concealed under his coat, Heck kept his eyes closed and waited for the sound of approaching footsteps. He sat in the darkness, his whole body tensed for the fight he knew was coming, but he heard nothing, except for the sound of Jefferson snoring.

Raising his head, he stared into the darkness, but saw only the empty room. With his Colt in hand, Heck stepped onto the deserted boardwalk in time to see a dark figure rounding the corner behind the bank.

He quickly removed his spurs and ran down the street, cutting between the livery and the freight office next door. He carefully maneuvered around the crates and boards that littered the alley and turned onto the street a few yards behind the man he was following.

Border Street was a wide road that ran behind the main business district and was where the few men of wealth lived in beautifully constructed homes which sat behind short fences made of wrought iron.

The man strolled along the street as if he were on a Sunday walk, never bothering to look behind him. He stopped in front of the corner house, which was larger and more opulent than any of the others. From its gabled roof to the colorful stained glass set in the front door, the home was built to impress upon all who saw it the wealth of its owner.

Sliding the latch on the gate, the man prepared to walk through, but Heck's voice stopped him in his tracks.

"Don't take another step, Hank. I'm sure Horace would appreciate the extra sleep, and you and me have some talking to do."

"Heck? What are you doing here?"

"I would ask you the same thing, but I reckon I've got a pretty good idea. You came here to warn Horace about our plan, right?"

"No, you've got it all wrong. I come out here to relieve my deputy and keep an eye on Horace, that's all. You can't really think I'd be working for Horace Snow or that I would have anything to do with taking Miss Farber?"

Heck pulled the hammer back on his Colt and said, "Walk back to me, now. This isn't the place for a discussion, but don't worry, we'll have time enough for that. Now, do what I said and walk over to me."

"What are ya going to do, shoot me? That would wake the whole street, and you'd have a hard time explaining my being dead. Horace has a lot of power in this town and he'll see that you all hang."

Heck knew that Hank was right. He had very little in the way of proof, and Horace had the money and influence to sway the law to do his bidding, however, none of this mattered much to him. "Hank, you're a gutless traitor and I hate traitors. It might cause me some problems, but you'd be dead, and right now that's sounding like a pretty good idea."

It took Hank only a moment to see things Heck's way, and he walked towards him. "Alright Heck, don't shoot. I'll do what you say."

"I figured ya might have a change of heart," Heck said, taking Hank's gun and shoving him down the street.

Chapter Twenty-Two

Heck had grown accustomed to betrayal and typically he reserved a certain mistrust for everyone, but even he was taken by surprise once in a while. Hank's betrayal was one of those times, and it left him feeling angry as well as foolish, but mostly angry.

Once the traitor had been locked away in his own jail, Heck, Jefferson and Digger then kept watch on Horace's house, but they didn't have to wait long for the banker to make his move. A few minutes after six in the morning, Horace rode out of his gate in one of the finest traps Heck had seen. It was not a practical conveyance for the terrain, and to Heck it was yet another example of Horace's arrogance. For the purposes of following him at a distance, the carriage couldn't have been more perfect, as the wheels made very distinctive tracks in the dirt.

"I'm sorry about Hank but dwelling on it ain't gonna do us any good," Jefferson said, as the three followed Horace out of town.

"Believe me, Jeff, my thinking is clear. This sort of thing is what I'm actually good at. Hank's treachery took me by surprise, but it's hardly worth shedding a tear over. He chose his side and he'll face the music, right along with the rest of 'em."

"What would make him choose to side with a man like Horace Snow?" Digger asked, not accustomed to seeing the treacherous side of people.

Heck wished that it was a lesson that Digger didn't have to learn. He liked the fact that there were still people who lived in a world of black and white, good and bad, but he was having to become a man fast, and he would have to learn the hard lessons early.

"Horace is a rich man and to a lot of people that's reason enough to take his part. Hank made the choice to sell his soul for easy money, but he'll be paying the price for that, just wait and see. No matter what he does from here on out, folks will know what kind of man he really is."

A few miles east of Uvalde, the tracks from the carriage turned down a narrow path. The trail was so overgrown with grapevines and honeysuckle that it would have been all but invisible, if they hadn't had the carriage tracks to guide them.

Tying their horses in a clump of trees, the three made their way along the trail, but stuck to the trees just in case a lookout had been posted. The mesquite and cedar trees grew close together and were intertwined with nettle and briars, which made for a slow and uncomfortable walk. While the others complained about this particular inconvenience, Heck took it as a good thing, as it made them take their time.

A half mile walk, along with numerous cuts and scrapes, brought Heck, Jefferson and Digger to the edge of the woods, beyond which lay a small pasture and a dilapidated single-story house. Horace's trap and horse were in front of the house, though there was no sign of its owner, or anyone else.

"Do ya figure Miss Farber is in there, Heck?" Digger asked.

"I don't know, kid, but I sure hope so," Heck said, looking at the house and surrounding area through his field glass.

"What's our play?" Jefferson asked.

"I'm trying to figure that out. Getting to the house means crossing seventy-five feet of open ground. If anyone in the house is standing watch, they'll cut us down before we get close."

"Let me go, Heck," Digger said excitedly. "I'm small enough to get up there without 'em seeing me."

"Don't be in such a hurry to meet your maker, boy," Jefferson said, pulling him back into the trees.

"Y'all stay here. I'm going to make my way to the other side of the house. Jefferson, you keep that front door covered with your rifle, and don't let the kid do anything stupid."

"And just how do ya expect me to do that? That boy ain't got enough sense to be scared."

"Just do your best and be ready to back my play. There probably ain't but one or two men with Horace and we still have the element of surprise on our side."

Forgotten Country						John Spiars

    Heck hurried through the trees and brush to the far side of the house. The remnants of a barn stood between Heck and the house, and he saw that it would provide the cover he needed to make his move unseen. The front wall and most of the roof of the barn were missing, making it little more than a lean-to, but it provided enough of a shelter for Horace's men to keep their horses.

    Giving a quick glance around the area, Heck ran from the safety of the trees and made it to the barn, quickly ducking inside. His sudden appearance startled the two horses inside, causing them both to let out a loud whinny that Heck was certain must have been heard inside the house.

    Afraid that his presence had been detected, Heck ran from the barn and charged the house's side door, which was no more than thirty feet distant. As he approached, the door swung open and a man stepped out, almost running into Heck. Startled to find someone standing so close to the house, the man jumped backwards and threw his hand up, firing wildly into the air.

    Ashamed of his reaction, the man regained himself and attempted to set up for another shot, but in the moment of truth one rarely gets a second chance. Heck knew before the shot left the man's gun that it was wasted, and he also realized that he would have to kill him.

    The man wore a flat-brimmed hat with a tall crown, which was battered and stained by much wear in all sorts of weather. His shirt and britches both sported multiple patches where holes had been mended, which was a considerable amount of work to go through, unless one didn't have the price for new clothes. Heck had been around enough cowboys to recognize one when he saw them, and if the man's appearance didn't give him away, his lack of skill with a gun certainly did.

Heck had to admit a certain admiration for the cowhand. Instead of running or giving up, the man stood his ground and tried to get off another shot. Regardless of his respect for the man, Heck had no intention of dying at his hands. Raising his Peacemaker in front of him, Heck fanned three shots, driving the cowboy back inside the door and knocking him off his feet.

"Those were shots," Digger said, jumping to his feet. "Heck's in trouble." Not waiting for instructions, he pulled his pistol and ran toward the house.

"Dang it kid, get back here," Jefferson called angrily.

He thought about chasing after Digger, but movement on the house's front porch captured his attention. With the skill of an experienced hunter, Jefferson brought his Henry to his shoulder, and quickly flipped up the guns ladder sight.

Two men exited the house and looked around in a panic for the source of the gun shots. Running for the porch, one of the men, dressed in a dark suit and sporting a bowler hat on his head, tried to make his way to the horse and carriage still standing in front of the house.

The other man, dressed in old, weather-beaten clothes, headed for the side of the house. As he stepped off the porch, he ran into Digger, and both were knocked to the ground.

It took Digger and the other man a moment to collect themselves and realize what had just happened. As they stumbled to their feet, they became aware of each other and both raised their pistols.

The cowboy was the first to bring his gun into play, firing a shot at Digger from no more than five feet away, but the Lord was not yet ready to call Digger home, and the shot missed to his left by only inches.

Digger fumbled with the Walker's stiff hammer but finally managed to lock it back and fire. In his haste, he jerked the trigger, causing the forty-four caliber ball to miss its target and strike one of the wooden posts supporting the porch.

Cursing each other while lining up a second shot, the two extended their pistols out in front of them, so that the barrels were only a few inches away from each other and prepared to fire. They stared into each other's eyes, acknowledging that one or both of them would soon be dead. They both took a deep breath and then slowly exhaled, each man seemingly frozen in time, engulfed by the silence that seemed to emanate straight from the grave.

A shot echoed through the trees, shattering the unnatural silence, causing both opponents to be shaken from their trance-like state. Digger slowly lowered his pistol to his side, watching as the life seeped from his enemy's eyes at the same time the blood seeped from his body. The cowboy took a couple of shallow, raspy breaths before leaning to his right, and then finally falling to the ground.

Horace fumbled with the reins as he tried to coax his carriage forward, but the gunshots and loud voices panicked his horse and it refused to budge. The gunfire and the sight of a man being killed in front of him hadn't done Horace's nerves any good either, and he felt as if he might lose his breakfast.

Giving up, Horace climbed out of the trap and tried to make his getaway on foot, but like gun battles and the sight of blood, physical activity was not something he was accustomed to. After falling on his face, he only made it a few feet before he heard the unmistakable sound of a rifle being cocked behind him.

"Hold it right there, Horace," Jefferson said. "I've already killed one man today, so let's not make it two."

"Please don't kill me," Horace pleaded. "None of this was my idea and I haven't hurt anybody."

"Why don't we find Miss Farber and see what she has to say. If you've done anything to her, I expect my brother will be hanging ya from the nearest tree."

Stepping over the body of the dead cowboy, Heck entered the house. Ejecting the spent cartridges, he slid three new shells into his Colt as he carefully began searching for Caroline.

The house was small, with only two rooms, and he quickly determined that she was in neither one of them. His heart sank as the realization hit him that Caroline must have been killed. He cursed himself for ever believing otherwise, and suddenly he wished he had treated the cowboy to a slower death. He wanted answers, and he figured Horace Snow was just the man to provide them. He didn't think the skunk would spill his guts willingly, but Heck was already thinking of ways to loosen the banker's tongue.

Heck knelt down on the houses dirty floor, contemplating the things he would do to Horace, but at the same time trying to gain control over his emotions. As his mind wondered down a dark road, a sound much like that of rain hitting wood caused him to rise to his feet in search of the source.

The sound drew him to the small kitchen, but as he stopped to listen, the house was once again silent. He looked around the room but saw nothing. Heck assumed the sound had just been a product of exhaustion, and shaking his head at his foolishness, he looked down and saw a cutout in the floor of the kitchen.

Heck dropped to his knees next to the cutout and saw that there was a handle attached to it. Taking a deep breath and saying a quick prayer, he drew his pistol and pulled back the handle. The trap door creaked open, and even before he peered into the darkness, a scream cut through the black depths of the pit, and it was a voice he recognized immediately.

"Caroline, it's me, Jesse. I'm coming down to get you outta there."

Heck scrambled down the wooden steps to the bottom of the root cellar and was immediately embraced by Caroline.

"Jesse, is it really you?" she sobbed.

"Yes, it's me. You're safe now."

"I knew you would find me, Jesse," she said, as tears rolled down her face. She held him tightly and continued to sob uncontrollably.

As he held the woman he loved, Heck thanked the Lord for his mercy. He couldn't believe how quickly things could change. Just a few moments before, he was at the lowest depths he could imagine and now, in Caroline's embrace, he couldn't imagine being happier.

The morning sun danced off the damp grass as the rays trickled through the tree branches, and as Heck

Forgotten Country   John Spiars

stepped onto the front porch, he was sure he'd never witnessed a prettier start to a day.

Jefferson and Digger smiled broadly as they saw Heck and Caroline walking through the door. Neither had been certain of finding Caroline alive, and both breathed a sigh of relief that their quest had turned out so well.

"Are ya alright, Heck?" Digger asked. "We heard the shots and thought maybe they'd gotten ya."

"I'm good, kid. Let me introduce ya to Miss Farber."

"Please to meet ya, ma'am," Digger said, tipping his hat. "My name's Digger."

"Is Digger the name your mother gave you?" Caroline asked, giving the young man a skeptical look.

"No, ma'am. She named me Orville, but most folks call me Digger."

"Perhaps so, but I'll call you Orville."

"Yes ma'am," he replied. He didn't really know why, but having another woman call him Orville made him feel good.

"And this is my brother Jefferson," Heck said, pointing to his brother.

"It's a great pleasure to meet you, Miss Farber. My brother has spoken of you many times. I hope you're doing okay despite your ordeal."

"I believe I will survive. Thank you, Jefferson."

"What happened out here?" Heck asked, after seeing the dead man laying just off the porch.

"Jefferson saved my life," Digger said. "That fella would have killed me for sure if your brother weren't such a good shot with a rifle."

"The kid talks to much," Jefferson said modestly, "but we did manage to take this skunk alive."

Forgotten Country   John Spiars

   For the first time, Heck noticed Horace sitting on the ground with his hands raised above his head. The fear and sadness he had felt when he thought Caroline might be dead once again turned to anger, and with a rage he had always tried to keep buried deep, he made his way toward Horace. The banker's normally smug demeanor turned to fright as he saw Heck approaching, but it was Caroline he should have been afraid of. Before Heck could reach him, Miss Farber leapt in front of him, and with a right cross that would have been the envy of any prize fighter, she knocked him flat, loosening several of his teeth in the process.
   Not satisfied with merely one punch, she cocked her arm back to deliver another, but Heck managed to grab her arm and restrain her.
   "Hold on there," he said, pulling her back. "We need to get some answers out of him, and that'll be a lot easier to do if he's still conscious. It'll also make it easier to get him back to town if he can set a horse."
   "Well, ask him, but afterwards, I'll be wanting to have a few words with him myself."
   Lifting Horace to his feet with one hand, Heck got his emotions under control and suppressed the urge to finish what Caroline had started. "I hope you know a good dentist, cause you're gonna lose a couple of teeth, but I reckon that'll be the least of your worries. Ya see, we hang killers around here, and I figure the missing marshal is dead."
   The thought of being hanged for murder shook the banker to his roots and he began to sob. "I didn't kill the marshal, that was Hank. He wanted to be the new law in Uvalde, so he said he would take care of the marshal. Whatever happened to him was all Hank's idea. I just brought Hank into the plot in order to keep an eye on you."

"Yeah, and to kill me when the time was right," Heck said, shoving the man back to the ground.

"He wasn't supposed to kill you. He was supposed to lead you out here so that these other men could do it."

"Let's talk about these men," Heck said. "How do you know Mason Lorde?"

"I don't know who Mason Lorde is?" Horace said, trying hard to stifle his crying.

"Those dead men are cowboys and their horses are wearing the Flying L brand."

Horace Snow was an experienced liar, but he was also alone with men who would enjoy having any excuse to kill him, so his usual inclination to avoid the truth didn't seem to be the healthiest route.

"I was telling the truth. I don't know Mason Lorde, but I know of him. These two came to town and said that their boss needed a favor, and he would reward me with future business deals. All I had to do was give them a place to hole up and assist them with their plot to lure you to town. The marshal was a good law man and I knew he would be trouble, so I brought in Hank to get rid of him. I never wanted to hurt you, Caroline. I just wanted to get revenge on Mister Carson and I figured I could make a useful friend in Mister Lorde at the same time."

"Mason Lorde really wants you dead, brother," Jefferson said.

"No," Heck replied. "If he'd really wanted me dead, he would have sent one of his hired guns and not a couple of cow hands. He didn't care about killing me, he just wanted me out of town. We've gotta get Caroline and our prisoner back to town, and then we've gotta high tail it back to the ranch. I fear something will be happening, if it ain't already."

Chapter Twenty-Three

"Sheriff, you'd better just turn me loose," Earl Mosby hollered from his cell. "Mister Lorde will be coming to get me out. How long do ya think you'll be able to hold me?"

"Mason don't care about you," Sheriff Garhardt said. "I've known him longer than anybody, and I can tell you that once you're no longer of use to him, he will get rid of you permanently. It's just your good luck that I'm not about to give up my prisoner to him or his men."

"I don't believe a word you say, sheriff. You're a low-down traitor. Mister Lorde is your friend and you took the part of that bounty hunter scum? I'm gonna enjoy watching him kill ya, but then again, maybe he'll give me the pleasure of doing it myself."

"Son, I know you may be too dumb to understand, but I'm the only one standing between you and the grave digger, at least until you go before a judge. Now, if you'll excuse me, I've got to make my rounds."

Sheriff Garhardt walked the streets of Weatherford, waving to the patrons and tipping his hat to the ladies. He enjoyed the respect that the folks of Parker County had for him, and the pride he felt by providing them a safe place to live. The county had grown to be one of the wealthiest in Texas due in no small part to the law and order that Lars Garhardt provided. Drifters and outlaws had tried many times to disrupt the peace and prosperity of Parker County, but none had been able to stand up to Garhardt.

Sheriff Garhardt had the valuable skill of being able to judge men, and he knew that Mason Lorde was going places from the moment he met him. After the war, Lars had followed him to Texas in hopes of sharing in his wealth, and his plan had worked better than he ever dreamed. Lorde had ensured his election to sheriff and from that office, Sheriff Garhardt had kept the county in line so that he could build the largest and most profitable ranch in the territory. The Parker County Sheriff not only drew a handsome salary, but as the one who collected the taxes, he also got to keep a percentage of the money he collected.

He lived in one of the nicest houses in town and had managed to sock away a sizeable sum of money, but somewhere along the way, the badge and what it stood for began to mean something to him, more even than the money and his friendship with Lorde. As upholding the law had become more important than protecting Mason Lorde's interests, tension between the two grew to the point that for the first time he had worried about the upcoming election. While arresting Lorde's best gun hand would do nothing to mend fences with his former friend, it went a long way to making him feel like a real lawman, and it seemed to make the citizens of Weatherford happy as well.

His daily walk, as usual, brought him through the doors of the Wild Mustang Saloon, where he enjoyed a daily beer on the house.

"Good afternoon, Lars," a familiar voice boomed from across the room.

"Hello, Mason," Sheriff Garhardt replied. He knew he should have been surprised to see the cattle baron in town, but for some reason, unknown even to him, he wasn't at all surprised. "What are you doing in town?"

"I came here to talk to you, Lars. For old times' sake, I thought I would give you the opportunity to come back into the fold. You have been led down the wrong road, but it's not too late. All you have to do is open up the jail and let Earl go free."

Lars paid little attention to Mason's words. Instead, he looked about the room for any of his hired guns, but he saw none. It was early afternoon and the saloon only had a few customers, all of them local residents, except for Mason.

The sheriff picked up his beer and took a long drink, after which, he turned to Mason and said, "Mason, you're a rich man, and while you might own everything for as far as the eye can see, you don't own the law. As long as I wear this badge, I intend to uphold the law, even if that means going against you, my oldest friend."

Mason Lorde raised his glass to the sheriff and then downed its contents. "I figured you would say that, but I had to try. Since the days of Jesus Christ, there's only been one way to deal with a Judas."

Putting his glass to his lips, Lars finished his beer, but had he known that it would have been his last, he would have lingered over it a bit longer. The bullet from Mason's gun shattered the thick glass of the beer mug and entered Garhardt's body just above his stomach. The second shot was almost dead center of his chest and ended the sheriff's life instantly. Still clutching the glass handle of the beer mug, the sheriff fell backwards and hit the wooden floor with a hollow thud.

Mason Lorde flipped a coin onto the table and placed his nickel plated .45 back in its holster. To the barkeeper, he said, "Give him a proper funeral, but tell the county officials not to elect a new sheriff until I tell them who that shall be." Stepping over the body of his former friend, Lorde strolled leisurely out the door, whistling his favorite Irish ditty.

"How long you reckon it'll be before Heck and the others make it back?" Darby asked, as he and Ulley pushed the small herd of cows across the river.

Ulley didn't respond or even look up at the younger man, but instead, he kept his eyes on the herd, while his worn fingers expertly rolled a cigarette. He wasn't a man who liked a lot of chit chat while he worked. The cowboy life suited him precisely because it was mostly a solitary vocation, and most of those who pursued it were not given to idle talk.

"Hey old man, did ya hear what I said?" Darby asked. He knew very well that his companion had heard him, but he intended to needle him until he received a response. Darby had worked with Ulley long enough to understand his ways, but it rankled him to be ignored just the same.

Forgotten Country   John Spiars

"Yeah, I heard ya, but I didn't see the need to spoil a beautiful morning with a lot of useless talk. I don't reckon I know when they'll be back. In fact, I don't reckon on much of anything except getting these cows moved to the south pasture."

"Sorry to disturb ya," Darby replied. "I just thought a little conversation might liven things up a bit."

"That's the problem with you city fellers. Ya think things always gotta be lively and ya got no appreciation for the sounds of nature."

"I like nature just fine, but don't ya find it gets lonely out here? Wouldn't you like to see and talk to other folks some?"

Crushing out his cigarette, Ulley looked into the distance and spread his arms as wide as he could, as if he were taking hold of all that he saw. "Look at all that out there. Land as far as the eye can see. You've got green grass, trees, the river, and they provide everything a man could possibly need. You've got beauty to fill your mind, food to fill your belly, and the makings of shelter to keep ya dry. Everything that the Lord intended a man to have is right there. It won't always be like this though. One day, this will be gone, but I'll have seen it, and to me that's worth more than all the saloons in all the towns. But your different kid, you need all that noise. Why don't ya get a job in some town where a body can have all the piano playing and pretty girls he could want?"

Darby took in the same vista as Ulley and tried to see what the older man saw, but it wasn't there. Where Ulley saw life and beauty, Darby only saw emptiness and death. Taking a deep sigh, the young man said, "Heck saved me, and I ain't about to let him down. He needs me here, and here is where I'll stay."

"Suit yourself, but if you're staying, ya need to keep your mind on your work. Ya got a couple of cows beginning to trail off to your left."

Pulling the reins to the left, Darby trotted after the two strays. The first lesson he had learned about dealing with stock was that they had a knack for seeking out the most precarious situations and putting themselves right in the middle of it. The two strays he chased were certainly no exception, and they darted straight for a gulley wash that had been carved by recent flooding and was perfect for trapping stray cows that had more curiosity than sense.

Pushing the cows forward, Ulley watched over his shoulder as Darby disappeared into the wash. With his attention distracted, he did not see the three Slater brothers coming towards him from out of the trees.

With hatchets and knives raised, the three men charged Ulley at full gallop. The old cowboy looked up in time to see the blur of a horse and rider as Cain Slater rammed him, knocking him from his saddle.

Ulley landed on his back, the force of which forced all the air from his lungs, causing him to gasp and choke for a breath. Making it to his feet, he saw the brothers jump from their horses, and he realized he was in a fight for his life, one he was not likely to win.

Zeke Slater ran at the old man, but Ulley brought his pistol up and fired, catching the man in the shoulder. The bullet spun him around and with a cry of pain he dropped his knife. Ulley cocked his Colt and turned, but a blow from Cain's hatchet deflected the gun, causing the shot to be fired harmlessly into the dirt. Before he could line up a third shot, Cain's hatchet sliced across his chest, and then another cracked his skull.

Forgotten Country	John Spiars

As Ulley fell to the ground, Cain and his brother Devlin descended on the old man, chopping and hacking until the man at their feet was no longer recognizable.

Darby had managed to get his rope around one of the strays and was leading it out of the wash when he heard the first shot. Dropping the rope, he drew his pistol and galloped out of the wash. He watched as Ulley fell, and he spurred his horse in order to get close enough for a shot. His horse moved rapidly across the rocky ground, but to Darby it seemed forever before he was finally within range.

When he was within fifty yards, he pulled back the hammer and fired. The bullet did not seem to connect with a target and he fired a second and then a third, but as the three Slater brothers scrambled for their horses, not one of them appeared to be hit.

Darby reined his horse to a stop where the men had gathered, and he saw the bloody form of something he couldn't make out as human, but knew it had to be Ulley. He let the Slater brothers ride on, deciding it was best to try and help his companion, though at that moment, he wanted nothing more than to see the three men die at his hand.

As he knelt down, Darby knew that the old cowboy was beyond saving. The body had been butchered so that what was left lay in a pool of blood that was beginning to soak into the cracks between the rocks, and the hard soil had turned to a reddish mud.

He fought back the urge to vomit, not wanting to disrespect the man's memory by such an unmanly act of weakness. Gathering himself, he took both his and Ulley's coat and wrapped the body up for the long ride back to the house.

With his rifle laying across his lap, Darby led Ulley's horse, with the man's body slung across the saddle, back down the trail they had just travelled. There was no doubt a war was coming, but he hoped it wouldn't kick off in force until Heck and the others returned. In case he was forced to try and defend the ranch alone, he figured he'd better get Ulley planted in a proper spot quick, and then work on fortifying the house.

"That danged old cow puncher shot me," Zeke Slater complained, as Devlin prepared to dig the bullet out with a red-hot pen knife.

"You're lucky he didn't do worse than that, you fool," Cain chided. "Why did you let him get a shot off anyway?"

"It sure weren't my choice. Who knew that old man could be so fast."

"We sure slowed him down some," Devlin laughed.

"Yeah, I reckon his cow punchin' days are behind him," Cain replied.

Zeke let out a blood curdling scream as the hot knife dug into the bullet wound. His head swam, and he felt he would surely pass out from the pain.

"Keep quiet," Devlin said, hitting his brother with the back of his hand. "You cry worse than any woman I've ever seen or heard of. If ya want that bullet out, you'd better keep your mouth shut, or I'll leave it in there and watch you die from blood poisoning."

"You both need to keep quiet, and ya need to finish this business so we can get back to the ranch. Mister Lorde will be waiting to hear about this."

"Why didn't we just kill that green kid while we were there? He wasted most of his bullets shooting at us. The three of us could have taken him just as easy as the old man."

"Devlin, just shut up and leave the thinking to your betters," Cain said angrily. "Zeke almost got his self killed going after one old man who we had the drop on. Besides, that wasn't what Mister Lorde wanted. He's got other plans for Heck Carson and the others."

Chapter Twenty-Four

"What do ya think will happen to Hank and Mister Snow?" Digger asked, as the group waited at the San Antonio station for the seven o'clock train to Fort Worth.

"You can't tell what a judge's liable to do, but I reckon Hank will hang for the marshal's murder. Then again, they ain't got a body, so he might get off. Horace Snow ain't too popular, but he's got money, so he'll go free more than likely," Heck said, double checking his pocket watch.

"They should both hang, if you ask me," Caroline said, obviously still angry over the whole incident.

"It seems that the law isn't as persuaded by what they should do, as with the money of those involved," Jefferson said, waving his hand, as if pushing away the thought that the law ever acted impartially.

"Won't you come back to the ranch with us, Miss Farber?" Digger asked.

"Thank you, Orville, but no," Caroline Farber said. "I'm afraid that would not be proper. I will travel with you as far as Fort Worth, and then I will catch a train headed for Boston."

"Why do you want to go there? It can't be as exciting as Texas. Won't you get bored?"

"Boston is where I am from, and my family still lives there. You're right that Texas is exciting, but so is Boston. Just a hundred years ago, Boston was the birthplace of independence, and was also home to several of this country's founding fathers."

"But why do ya gotta go back?" Digger asked. "Heck really likes ya, and I know he wants ya to stay. Dang, he came all this way for ya."

"Digger," Heck snapped, "that's enough. Miss Farber is a grown person and knows her own mind, even if she is making a mistake."

"That will be quite enough from all of you," Caroline said. "I have been making my own decisions for many years and I will not be giving up that privilege to any man or boy. Now, as the train is approaching, I believe our conversation is at an end."

From the south, the T & P train could be seen making its way toward the station, followed by a growing cloud of white smoke. As it approached, the rhythmic chugging of the locomotive became louder, finally drowning out all other sounds under the covered seating area. With the hiss of the brakes, all those standing around the newly arrived train were engulfed in a cloud of steam.

"Thank you very much, gentlemen," Caroline said pleasantly. "I will see you all when the train arrives in Fort

Worth." Grabbing her carpet bag, Miss Farber walked confidently to the open door of the first car and disappeared up the steps.

Heck, Jefferson, and Digger took their seats on the train. The wooden bench offered no comfort other than the opportunity to sit and relax, which, after enduring the last several days, was just as good as a feather bed in the fanciest hotel.

"I don't understand why Miss Farber couldn't sit with us," Digger said with a yawn.

Half awake, Heck cocked one eye open and said, "It wouldn't seem proper for a woman to travel with two men and a boy. She'll be okay. I figure the lady is quite used to taking care of herself."

"That may be," Jefferson said, pulling his hat down over his eyes, "but it seems she's set on going back east. If you plan on a future with her, you'd better make your play soon."

"If she's set on giving up, I don't see there's much I can do. Besides, we're liable to have our hands full once we get back. Maybe it's better that she's going. I don't know what I'll have to offer her."

"Suit yourself," Jefferson said. "You never was one to listen to good sense."

Heck pulled out his pocket watch, and for the fifth time in an hour, he checked the time. "We have at least seven hours ahead of us on this train, and if it's all the same to you, I'd rather spend that time getting some sleep instead of talking about what I should or shouldn't do about Miss Farber. Taking advise from you and Digger about a woman is a little like asking the local Padre where to go for good whiskey."

"Yes sir," Digger said, "but I still say you need to get her to stay."

"Thank you, Digger," Heck snapped.

For the remainder of the train ride, the three said almost nothing, and slept for most of the time. Heck continued to check his watch and became more annoyed as time continued to speed by without them seeing any sign of their destination.

Finally, after being over an hour late, the train jerked to a stop at the Fort Worth train station. The passengers immediately jumped to their feet in mass and began pressing for the door, anxious to stretch their legs and begin the final leg of their journey.

"Let's go get our horses and gear so we can start the ride back to the ranch," Heck said, rising to his feet.

Jefferson blocked Heck's path with his arm and said sternly, "Digger and me will take care of that. You go speak to Miss Farber. Say what you must to get her to stay, brother, because if you let her get away, you'll regret it."

"You're just bound to keep at this, ain't ya? I'll go talk to her, if only to get you to shut up."

On the platform outside the train, the passengers pushed their way past each other, shouting and cursing as they tried to make their way into the building and on to their destination.

Heck caught sight of Caroline amongst the throng, and jumping to the platform, he made his way to her side just as she entered the T & P station.

"Caroline," he shouted, trying to be heard above the crowd. "I need to talk to you."

Stopping, she remained with her back turned to him. "Mister Carson, we really do not have anything to say to each other. I am going back to Boston and you appear to have a crisis that requires your immediate attention. Whatever feelings we might have shared were merely fleeting and unimportant when taken as a whole, and anyway, I believe mine were stronger than yours from the beginning. You enjoy the thought of love, but the moment it interferes with your ability to follow the wind, you throw it aside."

"That ain't true. Perhaps I have let my responsibilities interfere, but that doesn't mean my feelings for you weren't real. I have worked my whole life to make this territory a fit place for folks to live and build something and now I want to build something of my own with you. I love you, and I hope you will wait for me a bit longer."

"How long, Jesse? How long must I keep waiting on you to decide what you want?"

"I know what I want, Caroline," he said, gently placing a hand on her shoulder and turning her around. "I am building something for us here, but there are those who are trying to take it away, and I must settle with them. I have a friend who owns a place here in Fort Worth. It ain't exactly a proper establishment for a lady, but you will be safe there until I do what I gotta do. Please give me just a little more time."

"Alright, Jesse," she said finally. "I'll stay for a while, but not long. You do what you need to and then we'll talk about what comes next, but I have no intention of being taken for a fool."

The Lucky Panther Saloon was a short ride from the train station, but to Caroline Farber, it seemed like it was a whole other country. Located on the edge of Hell's Half Acre, the streets around the saloon were filled with gamblers, cutthroats, and drunks looking for a handout. Most decent folk wouldn't venture past Sixth Street, which was the dividing line between the business district and the Acre.

"This is where you plan on leaving me?" Caroline asked, as she watched a group of sporting women propositioning several cowboys who were stumbling along the busy boardwalk. "I would have been safer in Uvalde."

"The Acre is no place for a lady, I'll give ya that," Heck said, "but the place we're taking you is owned by a good friend of mine, and I promise, you'll be safe there."

The Lucky Panther sat at the corner of Seventh Street and Main Street and was the fanciest gambling house in the area. It catered to high rollers with the gumption and backbone to back their play. The finest French Champagne flowed from crystal goblets, and thousands of dollars exchanged hands with every turn of the cards. The smell of leather and oak mixed with the aromatic smoke that emanated from imported Cuban cigars, which were provided free of charge at each table.

The sight of three dusty drovers accompanied by a woman, caused much whispering and finger pointing among the well-heeled patrons and looks of indignation among those that worked there.

"We don't seem to be very welcome here," Jefferson observed.

"It'll be alright," Heck replied, pushing past the men in their tailored suits as he headed for the bar.

The bar keeper kept the drinks flowing like a man born to the job and was as quick with a surly comment as he was with the crystal glasses.

"Howdy, friend," Heck said. "Who manages this establishment?"

"I serve drinks, not information," he replied, "and it don't look like you or your friends have the price for even one. I suggest ya keep walking and find some other place to loaf. There are plenty of places down the street that don't mind taking in dregs."

"Mister, I've been as polite as I know how, and that goes against my natural inclination, so I will ask you one more time nicely. Who is in charge here?"

The man's jaw tightened in anger, but Heck's tone caused him to think a moment before responding. Unfortunately, his quick temper took control over his good sense. His hands dropped below the bar as he stared at Heck with eyes that seemed as though they might spew fire.

"Friend, if you're reaching for anything other than a drink for me and my companions, you're currently enjoying your last moment this side of the hereafter. This is a nice saloon, but it's not where I'd choose to die."

The anger in the bar keeper's eyes was suddenly replaced by fear, not the kind that keeps one from doing something foolish, but the type of fear that is felt when one has chosen a path that he knows will lead to his own destruction.

"Owen, put that shotgun down. This man's Heck Carson and he's a close personal friend of Mister Tillerson."

The voice startled the bar keep, but Heck noticed that he let out a deep sigh of relief after hearing the man's words. "Sorry, Mister Waubach. I thought he was just a bum looking for a handout. I didn't know he was Heck Carson."

"That's fine, Owen. Just get back to work. Mister Carson, I am Jean Waubach, and I am Mister Tillerson's personal representative here in Fort Worth. I manage his interests here while he is pursuing other ventures in Colorado. He told me I should expect a visit from you sometime, and I was to extend you every courtesy."

"Thank you, Jean, but I'm not sure I appreciate Red's lack of confidence in me."

Jean eyed the rest of Heck's group with curiosity, giving Caroline a warm smile. "Mister Tillerson speaks very highly of your abilities, though he believes you get yourself into trouble by sticking your neck out too much for others."

"Well, I ain't looking for help for myself, but for Miss Farber here. It may be that we've got some trouble coming our way, and I want her somewhere safe."

Jean looked at Caroline again and then back to Heck. "Miss Farber is welcome here for as long as you need, but what about this trouble you spoke of? Do you need some men? I could have an army at your disposal at a moment's notice."

"No, thank you," Heck said. "Just keep her safe."

"Don't worry about that. Mister Tillerson's people are loyal. We would die for him, and we would do the same for her."

"I hope it don't come to that," Heck said, pulling Jean to the side, "but if I don't come back, put her on the train for Boston." Heck shook his hand, and when Jean drew his back, there were two twenty-dollar gold pieces in it.

Jean started to protest, but after a second thought, he put the coins in his pocket and said, "I will take her there myself, if it should come to that. Just make sure you are on the winning side."

"I'll do my best," Heck said. Taking Caroline by the hand, he led her a few steps away from the others. "Caroline, you'll be safe here. I would trust Red Tillerson with my life and his people are completely loyal to him. I will come back for you as soon as I have settled things."

"I don't know what the future holds for you and me, but I wish you well. Promise me you will do whatever you have to do to stay alive," she said, a small tear appearing in the corner of her eye.

"Don't worry about me. Stayin' alive is what I do best."

Chapter Twenty-Five

"Come on in, Earl," Mason Lorde said, ushering the gunman into his study. "I hope that traitor of a sheriff didn't treat you too harshly while he had you in his jail."

"Nah, it weren't bad," the killer replied, taking a seat in the comfortable leather chair opposite his employer. "Least ways, I've been in worse jails. I reckon that sheriff ended up getting the worst part of the deal in the end. The boys say you took care of him real good."

Earl Mosby looked around the study which was richly appointed in leather and dark wood and noticed the bookcase behind Mason's desk was lined with beautiful leather-bound volumes. Earl had never seen so many books in one place and couldn't believe that anyone would ever take the time to read them all.

"I don't usually take an active part in such things," Mason said, as he leaned back in his chair, "but Lars was a trusted friend and I took his betrayal very personally. That presents you and I with a problem though."

If Earl Mosby had not been so filled with his own self-importance, he might have been clued into a subtle change in Mason Lorde's demeanor. As it was, the gunhand couldn't see how precarious his position really was.

"Whatever the problem is Mister Lorde, I'm certain I can make it go away. I've learned that there are very few problems that can't be solved with Colonel Colt's equalizer. Killing the right person has a way of setting things right."

Mason leaned forward, and a big smile came across his face. "You've hit the nail on the head, Earl. That was the very solution I came up with myself. Come with me, I've got someone I want you to meet."

Standing up, the cattle baron led Earl Mosby through a door that opened up onto the back porch. As they stepped onto the wooden porch, Earl saw the Slater brothers and several others were gathered in the yard.

Heavy wooden torches, along with a couple of kerosene lanterns, illuminated the back of the big house, and as he noticed the man's expression against the glow of the fires, Earl could see they were privy to something he wasn't.

"What's going on, Mister Lorde?" Mosby asked nervously. "Why are all the boys gathered around?"

"Well, I thought this would be a good time for Cain, Devlin and Zeke to introduce you to their other brother, Charlie."

Forgotten Country   John Spiars

As if he were a stage performer waiting for the cue to make his entrance, Charlie Slater stepped from the shadows and stood just off the porch in front of Earl.

"Charlie Slater is one of your brother's?" Mosby asked, gulping hard as the words caught in his throat. He had, of course, heard of Charlie Slater. They were both in the same line of work, though Slater, by all accounts, had killed far more than Mosby.

"He surely is," Cain Slater said proudly, "though I don't reckon he's liable to admit it to many outside the family. Charlie, well he's a might ashamed of the rest of us, on account of him being famous and all. Pa always did say he got all the smarts in the family."

"You three are a sorry lot," Charlie said, turning to his brothers. "Y'all enjoy killing, while I don't do it unless I'm getting paid very well for it. It pains me to make an exception now, but Mister Lorde promised me plenty of work once I've helped him get rid of a problem."

"What problem is that," Mosby asked, though he already knew the answer.

"You," Slater said matter-of-factly. "He said once I kill you, I will be paid handsomely to kill someone named Heck Carson. It seems I've heard his name before, but I can't quite place it. Well, I'm all talked out, so let's you and me get down to business."

Earl Mosby had never doubted his ability to come out on the winning side of any fight, because he always knew he was faster and a better shot than those he faced. In fact, he'd always felt a tinge of sorrow for those he came up against, as he knew their life was about to come to an end. He had no such feelings as he stepped off the porch and into the yard though, for he realized it was his life that was about to end, and he certainly did not want to die.

"Why are ya doing this, Mister Lorde?" Mosby asked, looking at his former boss.

"It's simple, Earl. You are no longer of use to me, and I only hang on to what I need."

As he turned back to face Charles Slater, he saw the gunman shift his gun belt slightly to the front, where his silver-plated Colt reflected off the light from the torches.

"As a courtesy, I'll let you make your play first," Slater said in a calm tone.

Earl Mosby looked into the eyes of the hired gun and saw the unfeeling gaze of a predator who had tracked his prey and cornered it. He knew there was nothing left for the animal to do but move in for the kill.

Mosby moved his right hand to his hip, but never got to his gun. The first of three bullets tore into his body, killing him instantly. The other two shots were merely for show.

"What do ya think, Mister Lorde?" Charlie asked, as his opponent's body hit the dirt. "Do I have the job?"

"Without question, Mister Slater," Mason Lorde replied. "With you joining the outfit, no one will stop me from controlling the territory."

"Thank you, Mister Lorde, but I expect to be well paid for any killing I do. I'm a businessman, not a butcher like my brothers."

"Don't sell your brothers short," Lorde said. "They have proved themselves to be very valuable as well. I'm famished, so let's all go see what the cook has prepared for supper."

Chapter Twenty-Six

Heck, Jefferson, and Digger, in an effort to reach the ranch house as quickly as possible, cut across the western pasture.

"We need to get to the house," Heck said.

"We saw a few strays, but that don't mean there's trouble. Besides, it ain't gonna do anyone any good if you go racing across this pasture and your horse steps in a hole. You'll be dead, but the trouble will still be there," Jefferson said. He knew something had happened but didn't think it wise for them to charge into an unknown situation.

"Ulley would never have left them cows scattered about like that. He may be a drunk, but he's too much of a cowboy to not go after strays."

"What do ya think has happened, Heck?" Digger asked.

Forgotten Country											John Spiars

"I don't know, kid, but I fear the worst," Heck replied. Unable to wait any longer, he set spur to horse and raced across the open field.

Galloping up the drive to the house, Heck knew right away that something wasn't right, in fact, nothing was right. It was the middle of the day and no one was outside tending to the daily chores. Even if Darby had gone to town, Ulley should have been busy working, or at the very least, sitting on the porch with a jug.

Jumping from the saddle, he slapped his horse on the rump, sending it out of the line of fire, and then took cover behind a tree himself. He shouldered his Henry and slowly began sweeping the front of the house but didn't see so much as a field mouse moving. The shutters were closed over the window, and the front door was boarded shut.

The first thing Heck had done after moving into the house was to cut gun slits into the shutters, and through these slits, he could now see the light from a lantern. "Hello in the house," Heck yelled. "Is anyone in there?"

Two rifle shots were the only response he received, and the bullets tore chunks of bark from the tree he was using as cover. Realizing the tree wasn't as secure as he had thought, Heck leapt from behind it and ran for the porch. Rifle shots tore up the ground at his feet, and as he dove underneath the porch, a bullet struck the ground where just seconds before he had been standing.

"Dang it, ya almost killed me with that last shot. It's me, Heck. Stop shooting."

"Heck? Is that really you?" Darby called from inside the house.

"Yeah, it's me. I'm gonna stand up, so don't shoot."

Darby opened the shutters and climbed out through the window. Relieved to see Heck at last, he ran to his side and began shaking his hand vigorously.

"It's good to see ya, Heck. I've been cooped up in this house for days, waiting for the attack, but I gotta tell ya, I'm sure glad I ain't gonna have to face 'em by myself."

"What attack? What are ya talking about? What happened here?"

"They killed Ulley. They cut him to pieces, and I figure they'll be here any minute to do the same to the rest of us."

"What do ya mean?" Heck asked, grabbing Darby by the shoulders. "Who killed Ulley?"

"It was them Slater brothers," he replied, pushing Heck away. "They ambushed him down by the river while we were moving cows to the south pasture. I was gone after strays when they attacked and by the time I ran 'em off, they had hacked Ulley to death."

"Did ya kill any of 'em? Did ya go after 'em?"

"I managed to run them off, but I figured it was best to look after Ulley than chase after the Slater's. I couldn't do anything for him, except bury him. That was three days ago, and I've been hold up here since then waiting to be killed."

"Grab me a couple boxes of .44 shells and a box of .45. I'm gonna have to saddle another horse, cause mine's pretty well spent."

"Sure thing, Heck," Darby replied. "Ya going after the Slater brothers?"

"That's my plan, but I'll be needing them bullets, so get moving."

"Stay where you are, kid," a voice called from the drive. It was Jefferson, who, along with Digger, had just rode up.

"I ain't got time to argue with you about this, brother," Heck said. "I need to be riding out while I've still got daylight."

"You better think about this before ya go off half-cocked," Jefferson replied. "They ain't attacked in force cause they got something else in mind. You should ask yourself what that might be before you ride out with a head of steam."

Heck knew what Jefferson said was right, but he also knew that there were times when a man had to take action if he was going to call himself a man. "They killed Ulley. They killed him because he worked for me. Would you have me do nothing?"

"I'm not suggesting we do nothing," Jefferson said, climbing down from his horse. "The first thing we need to do is round up those strays we saw. Then we'll take care of the other chores that have gone undone. While me, Digger and Darby are doing that, you can work on breaking those wild horses that are taking up space in the pasture. It's high time they started earning their keep."

Heck paced up and down along the wooden porch, a battle raging in his mind between what he wanted to do and what he knew he should do. "That's what you think our play should be? We should just work the ranch and let our enemies go? If we do that, we'll not only be prey for Lorde and his men, but any other cattle thief or cutthroat that has a mind to take what we've got. Weakness only encourages those given to evil deeds, and I'd rather take the fight to Lorde now, than have to fight all those that might come along who think we're easy pickings."

Putting his hands on his brother's shoulders, Jefferson said, "You say you want to be a rancher, well here's your chance. We tend to business here first, and then we take care of Lorde. If the work here ain't done, you'll lose this ranch without Lorde firing a shot, and then Ulley will have died for nothing. This will also give us time to think things through properly and figure out what our next play should be. That's the way I see it anyhow, but you're the boss."

Putting off dispensing the justice that Lorde and his killers had coming went against Heck's grain, but he couldn't deny that his brother was making good sense. "I reckon we best get our horses fed and then ourselves. We've all got a lot of work ahead of us in the morning."

Two weeks of hard, backbreaking work and the ranch was finally back in good order. While Jefferson, Digger and Darby mended fences, repaired the roof of the smoke house, dug a new well, shoed horses, and repaired worn out tack, Heck worked from sun up till sun down breaking the wild mustangs that they had brought up from the Hill Country. By the time the others had caught up on all the chores, he had saddle broke three fine horses and halter trained two others. He figured they would all make fine cow horses, but one in particular, a buckskin of about fifteen hands, he had in mind for Digger. Heck saw something in the boy that reminded him of himself, and he felt a future rancher should have a proper horse. Digger would grow into a good cowboy and should have a fine horse to grow into it with.

"That's some mighty good venison, Jeff," Digger said, as the four sat around the table, fatigued but alert enough to enjoy a good supper. "The beans are good, too. I ain't usually powerful fond of beans, but I sure like the way you serve 'em up."

"Thank ya, kid. The secret is bacon and molasses. They give the beans flavor, but I'm afraid we'll have to do without both. We're running low on most everything, including coffee."

"I reckon I'll need to make a run into town for supplies. This spread can run fine on prayer and just plain stubbornness, but it won't last a day without coffee," Heck said, savoring a cup of piping hot mud.

"You're right about that," Jefferson said, "but don't ya think that's a job better left to someone else?"

"I ain't sending someone else and maybe getting them killed too. I'm going and that's all there is to it."

"Fine," Jefferson replied, "but I'm going with you, and we'll be going to Weatherford, not Ellsby."

"Whatever you say, Jeff. It would seem you're the real boss around here."

"Maybe we should all go," Darby said. "I mean, if there's gonna be trouble, it would be better to have four guns instead of two."

"No, I don't want the boy involved in this, and I need you to stay here with him," Heck said.

"Heck, I ain't no boy, and I can take care of myself," Digger exclaimed. "I don't need somebody looking after me."

"No matter what everyone here might think, I run this ranch, and I say what goes and who stays. Me and Jefferson will leave at first light, and Darby and Digger will stay here. If that's too much to take, I'll pay ya what I owe and see you off my land."

No one spoke up and the rest of dinner was spent in silence. Everyone was aware that if they stayed, it would eventually mean they would be forced to fight for their lives. While Jefferson hoped the tension would pass with time, the rest wanted to get with it and have it done.

The next morning, as Heck and Jefferson hitched up the buckboard, Darby and Digger walked out of the barn, leading their horses.

"What do y'all think you're doing?" Heck asked, the anger in his eyes even more evident than that in his voice. "I thought I made myself clear last night."

"You did," Darby said with a smile, "but Digger and me didn't get the chance to do the same. We talked about it after dinner and decided that we're going with ya, and if you want to fire us you can, but we'll still be riding into town with y'all."

"You saved me, Heck," Digger said, "and I'm gonna be sticking by ya till I return the favor, no matter if I work for ya or not."

Heck went back to helping Jefferson with the wagon without saying a word. When they had finished, the two brothers climbed onto the wooden seat and directed the team down the drive. With a wave of his hand, he signaled for Digger and Darby to follow.

CHAPTER TWENTY-SEVEN

As Heck and Jefferson rolled through downtown Weatherford on their buckboard, neither man could believe their eyes. The once sleepy, prosperous town now looked like Dodge City on a Saturday night. Drunk cowboys roamed the streets, exchanging curses with one another and yelling hoots and cat calls at the few ladies brave enough to walk the streets unescorted. Rough types and assorted vagabonds slept off the previous night's carousing in front of the once beautiful courthouse.

"What do ya think has happened here?" Jefferson asked, pulling the Greener to within easy reach.

"I can't imagine," Heck replied, "but we'd better find Sheriff Garhardt and ask him."

Frightened townspeople ran across the street, narrowly avoiding being trampled by the careless men on horseback who galloped in every direction. Several times Heck had to pull back on the reins to escape a collision.

After finding a place to park their rig, the four walked along the boardwalk toward the sheriff's office. Gunfire echoed through the streets and blended with the distant cries of distressed citizens whose idyllic lives had come to an unexpected halt.

"Mister Carson. Heck Carson."

The voice that called his name was unfamiliar, and by the time Heck turned to face the stranger, his pistol was cocked and ready for action.

"I'm Heck Carson, but I don't know you, so I suggest you speak fast."

"My name is Bob Castleberry, and I'm the county judge for Parker County. I'm not armed, so I would appreciate it if you'd lower your pistol."

"Pardon me for saying so, judge, but this don't seem like a place where it's healthy to go around un-heeled," Jefferson said, keeping an eye on the crowd of toughs who had begun to gather around them.

"You're right about that," Castleberry replied, "and that's what I wanted to talk to you about."

"What has happened here?" Heck asked. "Where is Sheriff Garhardt?"

"Lars Garhardt is dead. He was killed three weeks ago by Mason Lorde."

"Good afternoon, judge," Otis Lorde said, walking between Bob Castleberry and the Carson brothers. Behind him were the Slater's, who despite their typical shabby appearance, looked as though they owned the world.

"Hello, Mister Lorde," the judge said. "How can I help you?"

Otis looked at Heck and Jefferson, giving them a cold smile. "Me and my friends were just wondering why you was passing the time with these shiftless outlaws."

"We ain't outlaws," Digger shot back. "It's you and these three that are the no-good murderers."

"Watch your mouth, sonny," Cain Slater said, "or me and my brothers will cut your tongue out."

Darby pushed past Otis and threw a punch that connected with Cain's jaw, knocking the man flat on his back.

Devlin and Zeke Slater reached for their pistols, but they were better with blades than guns and Darby, Digger, and Jefferson had their guns drawn while the Slaters were still trying to fumble theirs out of the holster.

Otis made a play for his own Colt, but he was no match for Heck, and found himself staring down the barrel of his Peacemaker.

"If you boys want to push this, we can settle this war right now," Heck said. "I think me and my friends would all sleep better if we just planted y'all right here."

"I'd think about that first," Otis said. "The good people of Weatherford might not take kindly to you killing their new sheriff."

"What are you talking about?"

"After the election next week, I will be the new sheriff of Parker County, and my first act will be to round up you and your friends. After a quick trial, it will be my pleasure to walk all of you up the steps of the gallows."

"That's all the more reason to finish 'em now, Heck," Darby said. "If he's elected sheriff, there'll be no stopping Mason Lorde."

"I'm with Darby," Digger said. "They killed Ulley and they'll do the same to us." He kept his gun trained on

Zeke Slater, hoping that the man would make a move that would give him an excuse to shoot him on the spot.

"Your mouth is about to get you in more trouble than you can handle, boy," Charlie Slater yelled. The crowd parted as the man walked down the middle of the street. The silver spurs attached to his highly polished boots jingled as he walked, but it wasn't a pleasant sort of a sound, but more akin to a funeral dirge. It wasn't just his spurs, but the man's whole being that gave the impression of death. With the collar of his frock coat turned up and his hat pulled down low, he looked like a cross between an undertaker and the angel of death. His pearl handled Colt set high on his hip in a cross-draw holster, and though it wasn't in his hand, anyone with knowledge of such things knew that could change in the blink of an eye.

"Who are you, mister?" Heck said, turning his head to have a look at the stranger, "and why are you taking the part of these no-account skunks?"

"My name is Charlie Slater and these three are my brothers, but they don't give me much to be proud of. I have recently come into the employ of Mister Lorde, and my first duty is to get rid of you. You have the reputation of being fast with a gun, so I'll be enjoying putting you in the ground."

"You've got quite the reputation yourself, Mister Slater," Heck replied. "Let's you and me settle this business here and now. I don't believe in putting off till tomorrow those I should kill today."

"We ain't killing nobody today, Heck," Jefferson said. "We're gonna walk away and get the supplies we came here for."

"That's the wrong call, brother. We can end this today and get back to the business of ranching. I don't care to keep looking over my shoulder waiting for one of them to shoot me in the back."

"Don't ya see what's happening here? Lorde wants to push us into a fight, where we'll either get killed or he'll have the excuse to hang us for murder."

"If I can interrupt," Bob Castleberry said. "I have a proposition that might solve all of our problems, but you will have to walk away from this now."

Heck uncocked his pistol and slowly placed it back in its holster. "Alright, boys, put your guns down. We're gonna go and find out what Judge Castleberry has up his sleeve."

"You disappoint me, Heck," Charlie Slater said. "I thought we were gonna have some fun, but that's alright. I'm a patient man."

"Be careful, Slater," Heck said. "When we finally do have it out, you might really be disappointed."

Walking up the steps of the sheriff's office, it was evident that it had not been spared the destruction that had been wrought on the rest of the town. The front door had been ripped from its hinges and was leaning against the door frame. All the glass in the windows were broken, and the wood porch looked as though someone had barely managed to put out a fire before it engulfed the whole building.

"Didn't the sheriff have any deputies?" Heck asked, stepping over the debris that littered the interior of the office.

"He had several," the judge replied, "but most of them left town shortly after Sheriff Garhardt was killed."

"What about the others?" Jefferson asked. "Are they still around?"

"No, but let's not talk about that right now," Judge Castleberry said. Pushing through the trash and broken pieces of furniture, he found several chairs and offered them to the men. "Mr. Carson, let me get to the point. This county needs a sheriff, a real one, not Mason Lorde's brother or one of his hired killers. As you can see, it will take an experienced lawman to clean this town up, and one who has, well let's say, a special interest in making things better. I believe you are that man, and I hope you will consider taking the job."

"Thank ya, judge, but I'm a rancher now, not a lawman. I should have taken care of business back there and everybody's problems would have been over, but I didn't, so the only thing I aim to do now is get the supplies I come here for and get back to my ranch."

"We need a sheriff not a gunhand, Mister Carson. As you can see, we have enough of those," Judge Castleberry said. "Thank you, gentlemen for your time."

"Wait a minute, judge," Jefferson said. "My brother spoke too fast. He would be proud to run for sheriff."

"No, I wouldn't," Heck said. "I've got a ranch to run."

"Me and the boys can handle the ranch work, right?"

"We sure can," Darby replied.

"You need to be sheriff, Heck," Digger said. "We'll take care of the ranch."

Heck stood up and walked to the window. Staring through the bars and broken glass, he watched as men on horses charged down the street, and panicked citizens moved out of the way before being run down. The bad element was taking over, and the bravest folk were scared for their lives. He knew it wouldn't be long before the good people left town all together, leaving only the outlaws behind.

"What do ya think one man can do?" Heck said, turning away from the window. "It'll take an army to clean this town up."

"Then we'll find us an army," Jefferson said, "but you need to do this. If you want to be rid of Mason Lorde and his men, then this is the way to do it, working for the law, not for yourself."

"Okay, judge. If I agree to this, what do I need to do?"

"Just be in town next Tuesday for the election," Judge Castleberry said. "I will get your name on the ballot and spread the word about who to vote for."

"I'll be here on Tuesday, but I hope we can find that army, or we'll all be facing a heap of trouble by ourselves."

Chapter Twenty-Eight

On election day most of the citizens of Parker County were in Weatherford. Many were anxious for the election returns, but some were there only to see the war that was certain to erupt.

In the saloon, the whiskey and beer flowed freely, thanks to Mason Lorde, who knew the best way to appeal to the voting public. For those who could not be swayed by the offer of free liquor, he had instructed his men to use both the threat of violence and violence itself. His hired thugs were positioned all over town so that the populace would not forget what could happen if the election didn't go for Otis Lorde.

Heck spent the day of the election giving speeches and shaking hands, two activities that went against his nature. It wasn't so much that he didn't like people or didn't enjoy talking, but he had always been uncomfortable talking about himself and it simply rubbed him wrong to tell folks why they should vote for him. By the end of the day, he had switched from telling people to vote for him, to talking about what the county could be if it had proper law and order, and what would happen if Otis Lorde were elected.

After the polls closed, Heck returned to the Weatherford House Hotel to rest and quench his thirst with a beer or two. He had never been interested in holding any kind of public office, but as he sat over his steak and fried potatoes, he found that he was too nervous to eat. Part of it was undoubtedly what was at stake in the election. If Lorde prevailed, it wasn't just his interests that would be hurt, but those of every small rancher and merchant in the county. Beyond these concerns though, was just the simple desire to win, to be the one chosen to bring law and order to the area. He hated to admit it, but he really wanted to be chosen as the best man for the job, especially since it would mean that the voters had put aside the threats and their fears to choose him. What he tried hard to put out of his mind was how he would go about cleaning up the town. He figured that could wait until he was elected.

"Now that is a sour face if I ever saw one. I reckon politicking just don't agree with ya, but I guess that just means you're honest after all."

Heck recognized the voice but knew that it couldn't possibly be him. As he looked up from the table, he was shocked to see the buckskin clad form of his old friend, August Wells.

"I'll be danged," Heck exclaimed. "August, is that really you?"

"What's left of me, anyway," he replied.

Forgotten Country   John Spiars

Embracing his friend, he still couldn't believe it was him. "What are you doing here?"

"We got word that you'd gotten yourself into a peck of trouble, so we decided to come down from the high country and bail ya out."

"We?" Heck asked. "Who else is with ya?"

"You didn't think we'd trust the old man to make it down here by himself, did ya, kid?" Jim King said, walking through the door, followed by Red Tillerson.

"This is quite a town you have here," Red said. "It makes Fort Worth seem like Paris, France."

"I can't believe you fellas are here," Heck said, shaking the hands of each man.

"These boys have been pushing me so hard, they ain't even given me a chance to have a drink in days," August said. "So, if we're gonna keep this conversation going, you'd better show me to the whiskey."

After the whiskey had been poured, the four men sat down at a table to talk.

"I'm gonna ask one more time," Heck said. "What are you boys doing here?"

"My man in Fort Worth, Jean Waubach, telegraphed me that you had shown up with a woman you wanted to hide out. He also said that you were in trouble with one of the local money men. I've come to the realization that you will be the death of me, so I decided not to just wait around for it to happen. August and Jim decided their lives had become too safe as well, so here we are."

"I'm mighty glad to see you fellas, but I fear this may be more than even we can handle. I've already dealt myself in, but I can't ask y'all to get involved. I'm running in the election for sheriff, but whichever way it goes, a shooting war is liable to start. If I lose, we'll have the full force of the law against us, and if I win, Mason Lorde will likely be out to kill us all as quickly as he can."

"Who is Mason Lorde?" Jim asked.

"He's a local cattle baron who's got his mind set on controlling this whole territory. He's already killed my ranch foreman and gone after a woman in an effort to hurt me. Her name is Caroline Farber, and she's the one that I've hid out at Red's place."

"You certainly are a glutton for punishment," Red said, downing his whiskey and refilling his glass. "Starting a ranch, running for sheriff, going to war with a cattle baron, and on top of all that, you've gotten yourself involved with a woman. If you had just listened to me, you'd be a rich man today and your only worry would be where to spend your money."

"I suppose I ain't as smart as I'd like to be, but I'm gonna build my life here, or die trying. I can't ask you to throw in with me, though, so if I were y'all, I'd ride on outta town."

"Nonsense," Red replied. "We've come all this way, so if I can't talk you into riding out with us, I suppose I've got no choice but to stay and help you prevail."

"For once Red is right," Jim said. "I didn't save your life all those times back when we were Rangers just to let you be killed by some no-good cattle baron. Since the gold and silver dried up in Oro City, life there ain't too exciting anymore, and even I'm getting bored."

August looked out the window, as though he were searching for something long since lost, something that he had no hope of getting back. "Well, I for one have no desire to die peacefully in my bed. You and I fought side by side in many engagements during the war and after, and we've always managed to come out on the winning side. I would be proud to fight alongside you once more, even if we're meant to come up short this go around."

"Alright then," Heck said. "I reckon I've got the army I was needing, so I suppose there's nothing to do but wait and see how this voting goes."

"You ain't gotta wait anymore," Jefferson said, walking into the room breathlessly. "The counting is over and you're the new sheriff."

"Are you sure about that, Jeff?"

"That's the same thing Otis Lorde asked, and yes, they counted 'em twice."

"Well, boys, I reckon I've got a lot of work to do," Heck said. "If y'all don't want to deal into this, I'll understand, but if you're gonna stay, I can sure use your help."

"We're all in, kid," Jim said, "so just tell us what ya want us to do."

"If these men are here to help, don't ya think you should introduce me?" Jefferson said.

"Of course, Jeff, pardon me. This is Red Tillerson. He owns the saloon in Fort Worth where we left Miss Farber. The ragged gentleman to my right is August Wells. Him and I covered some miles during the war, and a lot more after. Jim King you know. You met him in San Antonio. They might not look like it, but they are the army we've been waiting for."

"It's a good thing, cause Lorde and his men are in the street, and they're itching for a fight," Darby said, entering the room and looking more than a little green around the gills.

"How many of 'em are there?" Heck asked, as he stood up and began checking his gun.

"There's at least ten, but I would count on there being a few others in the shadows."

"Where's Digger?"

"He's watching the street, but don't worry, I told him to stay low and not start any trouble."

Satisfied that his pistol was loaded and in good working order, Heck placed it in his holster and walked fast toward the door. "That boy is head strong and not given to following orders. We better get out there."

"You can't go out there yet, Mister Carson," Judge Castleberry said, meeting Heck at the door.

"What do ya mean, judge?" Heck asked. "I'm the new sheriff, and now I gotta go uphold the law."

"You can't do that until I swear you in. It'll only take a moment."

Heck raised his right hand and repeated the words Judge Castleberry said, after which, a silver star was pinned to his chest.

"Congratulations, sheriff," Judge Castleberry said, shaking Heck's hand. "Now, go do what you have to, but try not to get yourself killed. I would rather not have to go looking for someone else to pin that star to so soon."

"Thank ya, judge. Let me introduce you to my deputies."

Chapter Twenty-Nine

"I reckon congratulations are in order," Otis Lorde said, as Heck and Darby walked up the street, "but I don't figure you'll be living long enough to enjoy the job."

Otis was joined on the street by the four Slater brothers and several men that Heck didn't recognize but figured to be more of Lorde's hired killers. The boardwalk was crowded with others that Heck knew worked for Mason Lorde, and he began to question the wisdom of bringing Darby along to face them.

"Are you sure you boys want to do this?" Heck said. "I won't have my back turned to ya this time."

"Are you ready to finish what we started the other day?" Charlie Slater asked, his hand resting on the pearl handle of his Colt. "I promised Mason Lorde I'd kill ya and I'm a man of my word."

"What if you don't?"

"What do ya mean by that?" Charlie asked. He was less surprised by Heck's question than the fact he didn't seem scared to be facing his gun.

"I mean, what if you don't kill me? What if I kill you? Will the rest of your boys ride out of town?"

"No chance," Cain Slater shouted. "None of you will leave this town alive. In fact, you and your friends won't be leaving this street alive."

"I figured you'd say that," Heck said, clapping his hands, "so I invited a few more of my friends to join us."

Everyone waited to see who would make the first move, when the silence was broken by the sound of four rifles being cocked at once. From on top of the roofs overlooking the street, Jefferson, Jim, Red and August appeared, aiming their guns at Lorde's men.

Two of Mason's cowboys eased their pistols out of their holsters and began to move toward Heck, trying to get in a position to fire on both him and Darby.

"I wouldn't do that if I were you," Digger said from behind them. "You'll be dead before ya get off a shot."

"Ain't you that kid that rides with Carson?"

"That's right," he said, pulling the hammer back on his Walker Colt, "but that don't mean I can't kill ya."

The two men didn't like the idea of being buffaloed by some stupid child, but they hated the idea of dying even more, so they carefully lowered their guns and placed them back in the holsters.

"Well, boys," Heck said, "I reckon we can all go to the devil together, or you can all drop your guns in the dirt and ride out of town."

Looking at the rifles aimed at their heads and then at Heck and Darby, Lorde's men began dropping their pistols one by one. Charlie Slater looked at Heck and wanted to kill him more than he had ever wanted to kill anyone in his life. He wanted to see Heck Carson laying in a pool of his own blood and choking in pain as he gasped his last breath, but he could see that would have to wait for another day. He was no coward, but preferred fights where the odds were a little more in his favor.

"We'll leave," he said, "but I promise you'll be seeing me again, real soon."

"C'mon, Charlie," Heck replied. "Why wait? Let's end this right now."

"It'll wait, but not for long," he said. "Enjoy your moment, Heck, cause you'll be dead and buried before long."

Lorde's men reluctantly turned and walked back down the street. Heck figured they were feeling the same as he would have in their position, and he knew they would be wanting pay back as quickly as they could get it.

"Follow 'em boys and make sure they actually ride outta town," Heck said, waving to the men on the roofs.

After keeping a vigil of the town through the night, the men gathered at the sheriff's office for a much-needed pot of coffee.

"I guess Lorde's men really left town. I didn't see hide nor hair of 'em the rest of the night," August said.

"They'll be back, you can count on that," Heck replied. "Hey Red, you ever heard of that Charlie Slater fella?"

"I've never had the pleasure myself, but I have heard stories. He made quite the reputation for himself in Kansas and Missouri, but from what I understand, he enjoys the killing more than the money it brings him."

"Why don't we go to Ellsby and take care of 'em instead of waiting for them to come after us?" Digger said, spitting his coffee back into his cup.

"Dang, that boy can't handle his coffee, but he's got enough gumption for three men," August said with a chuckle.

"We've got enough work to do here without going somewhere else looking for trouble," Heck said, swallowing his last sip of coffee and heading for the door. "We've got plenty of bad ones still in town, and they need cleaning out. Lorde's men will be back before long, but until then, we might as well deal with the outlaws we got."

"Well, I guess we best get to it," Jefferson said. "How do ya want to play it?"

Heck pulled his Greener from the rack and loaded it with buckshot. "We divide up the town and get rid of the scum. We'll fill up the jail cells first and then we'll start putting the prisoners in the corral out back. There's plenty of room in the cemetery for those that don't want to cooperate."

Getting to their feet, the seven men grabbed their guns and walked into the street to take care of business.

Walking through the bat-wing doors of the Dancing Sow Saloon, Heck ducked as a whiskey bottle flew from one side of the room to the other. A group of drovers were involved in a brawl, busting up tables and chairs, as well as each other. The drunken cowboys paid no heed to the presence of the new sheriff and seemed unconcerned about any interference from the law.

In a corner table, two saloon girls were doing their best to fend off three drunks who were pawing at them and ripping the colorful silk dresses they wore. No one cared about the plight of the women, who screamed while they did their best to keep their clothes from being ripped from their bodies. The only ones who even noticed what was happening were two men at the next table who seemed to be enjoying the spectacle, laughing and mocking the terrified screams of the defenseless ladies.

The only patrons who weren't involved in the orgy of wickedness were four of Weatherford's less prosperous citizens, who either couldn't afford the price of a drink or had already drank their fill. They lay huddled in a corner of the saloon and were snoring loud enough to be heard over the commotion taking place around them.

Making his way over to the two ladies, Heck knocked two of their attackers to the floor with the butt of his shotgun. The other two drunks stumbled over their own feet as they tried to come to their friend's aid but were no match for Heck. One was dropped to his knees as Heck swung his shotgun, connecting with the man's ribs, and the other was sent sprawling as Heck delivered a blow to the man's head.

"You ladies better get outta here," Heck said, escorting them to the door. "Where's the owner of this establishment?"

"His name was Wilbur and he was killed two weeks ago. With no law here, these men took over and have been holding us prisoner," one of the saloon girls said.

"Was it any one of them that killed Wilbur?"

"No," she replied. "The man that done it left town last night with the other men."

"Was it Charlie Slater or Otis Lorde?"

"It was Otis Lorde. Wilbur got drunk and said he wouldn't vote for him in the election. Otis didn't like that and just pulled out his gun and shot him."

"Thank you. You ladies go find someplace safe to hole up and don't come back here for a while. I'll take care of them that killed Wilbur soon enough, but right now, I've gotta deal with some business here."

"Thank you, sheriff," the two women said, relieved to be out the saloon and the nightmare that they had endured.

After they ran out of the Dancing Sow, Heck turned back to the other drunks and saw that his actions hadn't slowed their mischief down a bit. In fact, they didn't even seem to notice that he was there.

Heck raised his shotgun in the air and fired off one barrel, which startled the men and caused them to stop what they were doing.

"Good evening, gents," Heck shouted. He leveled the Greener at the crowd, hoping it would deter them from getting nervy. "I'm the new sheriff, and all of y'all are going to jail. I hope you'll come along quietly, but if ya want to do this the hard way, I'm alright with that too."

"You better learn to count, cause there's nine of us and only one of you," one of the men jeered.

"Maybe you should learn to count," Digger said, walking through the back door with his pistol drawn.

"Kid, you'd better put that gun down before ya hurt yourself," the man said, inching his hand toward his side.

Digger fired a shot at the man's foot, missing the toe of his boot by only inches. "It's you that's gonna get hurt if ya don't do what the sheriff told ya."

Seeing they were covered, and not wanting to challenge Heck's shotgun, all nine men instantly sobered up and dropped their guns.

Forgotten Country   John Spiars

After marching the men down the street, they were stuffed into a single jail cell, as Jefferson and Darby had already filled the other two.

"You only brought in twelve, we've already got eighteen and didn't have to go any further than the boarding house next door, which could hardly be called a reputable establishment," Jefferson bragged, happy to be one up on his brother.

"Don't get too full of yourself, we ain't getting paid by the arrest," Heck said, trying to disguise his bitterness at being bested by Jefferson.

"Your brother sure is a hard worker," August said, "but I've looked past that particular failing and decided to like him anyhow."

"I hope Judge Castleberry has gotten a good rest, cause he's about to be busy," Heck said. It was only his first day, but Heck was proud of the job they had already done. He knew they had a way to go to make the town a fit place to live, but he was looking forward to finishing and being able to go after Mason Lorde and his band of killers.

"Good afternoon, gentlemen," Red said, as he and Darby walked through the door of the freight office.

"Who are you and what do you want?" the man behind the desk grumbled.

"The owners of this business have sworn out a complaint against you and your friends here. They say you ran them out and have stolen their property, and while I'm on the subject of stolen property, I've also got some questions about those horses out there in the corral."

"You ain't answered my question, mister. Who are you, cause I'd like to have a name to put on your tombstone?"

"That's very kind of you," Red said. "I am currently in the employ of the new sheriff and you and your friends will have to come with us and go before the judge."

His comment caused the three men to burst into laughter, but after realizing that Red was serious, the smiles faded from their faces and they rose to their feet.

The man who had done all of the talking went for his gun first, but he had barely touched its walnut grip before the nickel-plated barrels of Red's matching Colts were pointed at his head.

The other two men contemplated reaching for their own pistols, but the sound of Darby cocking his gun caused them to freeze in place.

"Now that my friend and I have your attention," Red said, "do you want to follow us to the jail, or will the undertaker be taking you out feet first?"

"No, we'll be going along peacefully," the man said, gulping at the thought of how close he'd come to death.

"That's a smart decision," Darby said, shoving the men toward the door. "Now get moving and don't stop until you have reached the sheriff's office."

"You did very good, kid," Red said to Darby as they followed their prisoners out the door of the freight office. "You're wasting time working for Heck. If you want to plan for your future, you need to come and work for me. You will be running your own saloon in no time."

"Jim King," the voice from the street called. "I knew you when you was a Texas Ranger and you put me in jail down along the border."

"You'll have to do better than that," Jim said, loosening his pistol in its holster and stepping into the street. "I've brought in hundreds of no-accounts just like you, some under their own power and some slung over their saddle, but they all looked the same to me. What's your name?"

"I don't reckon it'll make much difference to you in a few seconds anyway. After you're laying in the dirt, I'll be having words with the new sheriff."

"I admire your confidence, but I doubt you'll be leaving this street alive," Jim said.

Without saying another word, the man reached for his gun, and while he would have been considered fast by most people's standards, he wasn't nearly quick enough to best Jim King. The former Ranger fired three shots into his chest and belly, which caused the man's body to jerk violently. He took several steps backwards before his legs gave out and he fell to the reddish-brown dirt.

"I tried to warn him," Jim said, to no one in particular, "but some folks just won't take good advice."

By the end of the first day, Heck and his men had filled up the jail and two corrals with prisoners. They took turns guarding their new charges, as well as making trips to the café for their meals.

Not wanting to incur the wrath of Heck and his deputies, the remaining bad element went into hiding, while the honest folk were still too scared to leave their homes. The saloons, gambling halls and bawdy houses were all closed, so the town was unusually quiet, and the men were able to catch their breath after a hard day.

"Not a bad start," Heck said, as he and the others gathered around a plate of fried chicken that the owner of the hotel had sent to the jail.

"We had a good day to be sure," Jefferson said, "but there's plenty of others that need to be brought in, and they ain't all gonna come along peaceful like. We've got a big fight ahead of us, and then we've still got Mason Lorde to deal with."

"That brother of yours ain't only a hard worker, but he's also got quite a gloomy side, don't he?" August said to Heck. "We're all alive and have this fine fried chicken to fill our bellies, so what do we have to be down in the mouth about. When you reach my age, you'll learn that sometimes that's enough. The only thing that could make things better would be to have a swaller or two of fine whiskey, and it just so happens I've got that covered as well."

"August is right," Red said. "We should be happy with the way things have worked out. There are two saloons and a boarding house that are just waiting for me to buy and return to the purpose for which they were intended. Once we finish this business with Lorde, the money will start rolling into this town and I aim to gather up as much of it as I can."

"As usual, our friend here lands on his feet," Jim replied, "but I reckon we've got some rough days ahead of us, so let's enjoy the here and now."

"Well then, let's have a drink to the here and now," August said, holding a jug of his special sour mash.

Chapter Thirty

"We've finally got us a quiet night," Heck said to Jim, as the two walked around town.

"Yeah, but it'll take the judge months to try all of them we got locked up, and no telling how long to rebuild the town."

"I know, Red is already trying to buy up everything he can get his hands on. I swear, we'll all end up working for him before he's done."

The men looked through all the windows and checked all the locks on the businesses along Main Street. After a few weeks, the merchants and those they employed were finally beginning to return and regular shipments of goods were making it into town.

"Things ain't apt to be quiet for long," Jim said. "There's rumblings that Mason Lorde has his men preparing for all-out war, and that they're getting ready to attack."

"I knew we'd have to deal with that sooner or later," Heck said, looking over his shoulder as a man on horseback trotted down the street, "but I was hoping we had more time, at least till we had this town back on its feet."

"Well I say, bring it. It's just like with the Comanche. If we've gotta go into battle, it might as well be now. After all, that's why August, Red and I come here."

"It sure was a surprise seeing y'all show up in Weatherford. I figured you were so set in Colorado, that you'd never leave."

"After the gold ran out, everyone moved on to Leadville, so we weren't leaving much behind."

"What about August? I thought he had married an Indian woman and taken up with her tribe. Don't tell me you two drug him out of a nice, warm tepee to come down here and possibly get himself killed."

"He won't talk about it," Jim said somberly, "but his wife and most of the tribe were killed. The army persuaded them to ride into Fort Carson for peace talks and then killed them all. August remained in Wyoming with several of the braves to hunt food for the winter, so he wasn't there. He decided he could either go to war against the US Army or come here and help a friend. He's still carrying a powerful amount of hate though."

"Dang, he ain't said a word to me about any of that."

"He doesn't talk to anybody about it, but he seems to drink more than he used to," Jim said.

"Yeah, I noticed that, but I didn't figure it was my place to say anything."

"This war of yours has been bad for you, but to tell you the straight of it, for Red, August, and me, it was the best thing that could have happened. It allowed us all to get back to Texas."

After making their rounds, Heck and Jim returned to the jail where they were greeted by Jefferson, Darby, and Digger, who's long faces told them something bad had happened, or was about to.

"Why the sour faces?" Heck asked. "You boys look like ya just came from a funeral."

"Not yet," Jefferson replied, "but if what we heard is right, we might be attending our own before long."

"What have you heard?"

"One of Red's people just delivered a message. Charlie Slater wants you to meet him on the street in Ellsby, supposedly to settle things, but Red figures it's a trap."

"Of course, it's a trap. They figure to get me and maybe a few others out of Weatherford, so they can attack, and then they'll kill the rest of us in Ellsby," Heck said, as he took his hat off and ran his hand through his thick but slightly graying hair.

"When do you think it will begin?" Digger asked.

"Unless I'm wrong, it's already begun," Heck replied. "Where is August and Red?"

"August is sleeping it off and Red is with his man that delivered the message, making arrangements of some sort."

"What do you plan on doing, brother?" Jefferson asked.

"I'm not gonna let 'em take this town without a fight, so I'm gonna stay here and do what I can, but the rest of you should leave. Y'all need to slip out of town and make your way back to the ranch. You'll have a better chance of making a stand there. The terrain's wide open and y'all could see 'em coming for miles. I don't mean to say it would be a sure thing, but it's the best bet."

"I ain't about to leave you here alone to fight all of 'em," Digger said. "If I'm meant to die, I'd just as soon do it now by your side."

"Nobody needs to die," Red, who had slipped inside without anyone seeing him, said with uncharacteristic optimism. "I've got a plan, so if you'd all care to listen, we might be able to live through this, and beat Mason Lorde as well."

"How much of August's corn squeezin's did you go through, cause you ain't makin' no sense," Jim said, certain that he and the others had come to the end of the road.

"As usual, while you do all the worrying, I've put my mind to more useful pursuits, such as coming up with a plan to solve all of our problems. So, if you will give me a few moments, I will try to explain it to you."

"Somebody should go wake up August," Heck said. "If everyone is gonna risk their neck, then we all need to hear Red's plan."

"I'll explain the finer points to the others, but you need to get ready to ride to Ellsby for your showdown with Charlie Slater."

"You mean for Heck to ride into Ellsby by himself?" Jefferson said.

"Yeah, they ain't exactly gonna be offering him a fair fight," Jim interrupted. "Even if he beats Slater, they'll kill him where he stands."

"I'm sure that is what they have in mind," Red said, "but that does not mean we're going to oblige them. Slater and Lorde will be counting on their numbers to win the day, and their overconfidence will be their undoing."

Forgotten Country   John Spiars

After listening to Red's plan, Heck began saddling his horse, while the others prepared to do their part. He wasn't at all sure that the plan would work, and even if it did, they could still lose a few of their number. While Heck thought the possible cost was too high, the others were willing to take that risk. He didn't like it, but he understood how the others felt, and taken as a hole, the vagaries of putting up a fight certainly held more appeal than just running away with their tail between their legs.

"I still say that going into Ellsby by yourself is foolhardy," Jefferson said, walking through the big double doors of the livery stable. "Why not let me go with ya? The two Carson brothers would be more than a match for any of them fools waitin' for ya."

"That's for sure," Heck replied, "but for Red's plan to work, all you boys have gotta stay here in Weatherford."

"I heard his plan the same as you, but he'll have more than enough men, even without me."

"I appreciate the thought, brother, but I'll be able to handle things alright by myself."

"You don't think I'd be able to help you, do you?" Jefferson said, in a tone that seemed both annoyed and hurt. "You believe I'd just be in your way."

"It ain't nothing like that," Heck replied. "You've got plenty of grit and backbone, but if this thing goes bad for me, I want to know that you'll be here to keep the ranch going. It's all I'll be leaving behind, and I want it in good hands."

"You don't need some plot of land for folks to remember you. Folks will know you were here because of everything you did to make Texas a fit place to live."

"They'll be remembering a legend not a man, and besides, I don't want to leave just a trail of men I killed, but something that I helped to build. So, I'll be counting on you to see that through for me."

"You're talking foolish anyway, Heck. You're gonna run through those outlaws in Ellsby like a knife through butter and be back here to make that ranch into something by yourself."

"I'm sure you're right, but I need ya here just the same."

"Alright, brother, have it your way," Jefferson said, clapping Heck on the back. "I'll be seeing ya back here when this thing is over."

"Sure thing, brother," Heck said, swinging his frame into the saddle.

Chapter Thirty-One

As he entered the town limits of Ellsby, Heck couldn't shake the feeling that he was riding to his own hanging. Red had explained his plan and it sounded good over a pot of coffee but the reality of it was some different. He trusted Red with his life, but he found it hard to believe fully in a plan he had no control over.

The streets were mostly deserted, except for the occasional shop keeper who gazed at Heck from the doorway of their business. Curiosity was getting the better of them now, but once the bullets started to fly, they would be hidden safely behind closed doors. While the decent people of Ellsby hated Lorde and his army of killers, Heck knew that at the moment they cared little about who would win the battle, and more about their own safety. In church on Sunday they may have prayed for deliverance from the cattle baron, but alone in the dark, when no one else could hear, their prayer was for the safety of themselves and their families.

A strong North Texas wind whistled through downtown, kicking up several small dirt devils that added to the eerie mood that had settled over the whole town. In front of the largest hotel in Ellsby, the street turned to the right, and as Heck rounded the corner, the finality of his decision was driven home.

Ten of Lorde's men waited, positioned shoulder to shoulder, blocking the road. Standing about ten feet in front of the others was a man dressed in all black that Heck immediately recognized as Charlie Slater. The man's coat blew in the breeze, revealing two pearl-handled Colts hanging on his hip in a cross-draw holster. Slater wore a pair of silver spurs on his black stove pipe boots, and Heck squinted as the sun reflected off of them.

Climbing from his horse, Heck tied the animal to the hitching post in front of the hotel, and then walked over to meet Slater.

"The others didn't think you'd come, but I told 'em you would. I'm glad you didn't make me look like a fool," Slater said. His mouth formed a slight smile, or at least the closest a man like Charlie Slater ever got to a smile.

"I see you've got a lot of friends with you. I must have misunderstood, as I thought this was going to be between you and me," Heck said, surveying the odds, and not liking what he saw.

"Oh, it'll be between us, but if somehow you should win, well, there's no telling what these men are liable to do. To tell ya the truth, I didn't think you'd be stupid enough to come here by yourself, but I reckon it don't make much difference now."

Forgotten Country   John Spiars

"Yes sir, you're surely right about that." Looking up, Heck caught sight of several objects glistening in the sun, and suddenly he was the one smiling.

One by one, Lorde's men noticed the reflection coming from the roof tops and strained their necks upwards trying to determine the source. Charlie Slater was the last to notice the commotion but was the first to understand what was really happening.

From each roof a rifle appeared, pointing down to the street, and each one aimed at Mason Lorde's men. Slater did a quick count of the riflemen but gave up in frustration after reaching twelve.

"As you said, a man would have to be a fool to walk into a situation like this alone. Now, I reckon you and I should get down to business," Heck said, pulling back his coat, revealing the stag grip of his own Colt.

"That suits me just fine," Slater said confidently, "but I want you to know that while you're busy dying here, your friends are gonna be dying on the streets of Weatherford. My brothers, Marshal Lorde, and a few of our other men should be arriving there about now, and my brothers are looking forward to cutting your brother into tiny pieces. Why, by the time they're finished with him, you won't—"

Heck, not wanting to listen to another word from the gunfighter, drew his Colt and ended the conversation with a bullet to the man's forehead. Charlie Slater's head jerked once, and the man stumbled back into the arms of his surprised comrades.

"Sorry about that boys, but I didn't think he'd ever shut up."

What transpired afterwards happened fast, almost by mistake, as those sort of things often do. One of the cowboys reached to his side, possibly going for his gun, but no one could say for sure. In the end, it certainly made no difference to him, a rifle bullet cut him down before anyone knew what had happened. Regardless of how it started, it erupted into a torrent of bullets that flew from both sides, though Mason Lorde's cowboys suffered the worst of it.

Most of the cowboys dropped their guns and dove for cover, but a few of the more fool hardy stood their ground, trying to fight it out against a superior force who controlled the high ground. They held out for a few moments, trading shot for shot, but in the end, they were all cut down, spending the last precious seconds of life watching the dirt around them turning red with blood.

"Stop firing," Heck yelled, walking to the middle of the street. "They're down, and the others want to give up. Don't ya, boys?" he said, pointing his pistol at the remaining cowboys.

Each one of Lorde's remaining men threw their hands up and nodded that they wished to surrender. A nice safe cell in the town's jail seemed a much better option than the one their friends had chosen.

The deaths on the street that day would live on in the memories of the townspeople and the stories they would tell their children and grandchildren. The tales and the written records would describe the aftermath in sufficient detail, but the old-timers would always be quick to point out that they did not begin to capture the true gruesomeness of the scene.

After seeing Mason Lorde's hired men to jail, Heck walked outside to thank the men who had come to his aid. Their leader was busy giving orders as the men picked up their gear and prepared to leave town. He carried himself with an air of confidence and authority which was the essential combination possessed by those in positions of leadership, and though Heck had only met him once, he would have recognized him anywhere.

"Jean Waubach, it seems you have come to my aid once again. Thank you for what you and the others did here today."

"You are quite welcome. I am indebted to Mister Tillerson, and he feels the same sense of debt to you. It is always tragic to be forced to take a life, but these men gave us no choice. I am afraid though that the battle is only half done. Weatherford at this moment is under attack, and my presence may be needed there."

"Let me get my horse and I will go with you," Heck said.

"No, Mister Tillerson was very clear. You are to remain here and hold this town. If Mason Lorde moves back in here, then everything that happens today will have been for nothing."

"But my brother and my friends are there, and I should be there for them."

"Whatever is going to happen will have already taken place by the time we get there. If our people have lost the day there will be nothing left to do but avenge their deaths, and my men and I are perfectly capable of taking care of that. You are the law and shouldn't be party to such things."

"Let's hope it don't come to that," Heck said, shaking Jean's hand once again. "Before you go, tell me how Miss Farber is making out."

"She is a strong woman and does not take well to living in hiding. I would never presume to tell you what to do, but if you care for that woman, I suggest you go to her as soon as you can."

"Thank you again for all you have done, and I will take your advice to heart."

Slowly the good people of Ellsby began to come outside, unsure at first, but soon realizing that they once again had their town back. After removing the bodies of the dead, they got down to the business of opening their shops and taking control of their lives.

Heck walked around town, shaking hands and introducing the citizens to their new sheriff. He found several men to volunteer as deputy marshals, establishing a sense of law and order that had been missing in Ellsby for a long time. He appreciated the gratitude of the citizens, but he wished he could be with Jefferson and the others in the shooting fight he knew they were now facing.

Chapter Thirty-Two

"How long do ya think we'll have to wait?" Digger asked, as he and August kept watch from the hotel window.

"How should I know, sonny? I ain't the brains of this operation. Red's the one with all the answers."

"But you think that Lorde's men will be attacking though, don't ya?"

"Oh, they're coming alright. You can bet your bottom dollar on that. I've been in enough scrapes to feel it in my bones when troubles on the way."

"Ya think Heck is okay? I should've gone with him. I mean, he rode in there by himself, and that Charlie Slater is a bad man," Digger said, wishing there was something to do besides just waiting.

"For such a young feller, you sure got more than your share of worry," August said. "Worrying over things that you can't change don't do nothing but burn a hole in your liver. I've covered a good many miles and years with Heck Carson, and there's one thing I can tell ya for sure about him, he's a man who can take care of himself. He's as fast with a gun as any man alive, and more than a match for Charlie Slater."

"Ya really think so?"

"I do," August replied confidently. "Slater talks too much guff, and I guarantee he can't back it up."

August knew that things didn't always work out that way, and that when it came to gunfights, anything could happen, but he didn't figure it'd do any good to burden Digger with that knowledge.

Looking down on the deserted street below, Digger felt a pang of loneliness seeing the emptiness where there used to be so much life.

"How did you and Heck come to know each other anyway?"

"Why do ya ask so many questions? That's what's wrong with people, they waste too much time thinking about what's dead and buried instead of enjoying today. I'd rather drink the corn squeezin's I got in front of me rather than remembering what I drank yesterday."

Digger wrinkled his brow and said, "I was just asking a question, but I don't know what it has to do with whiskey."

"Me, Heck and a boy named Tommy joined the Army together at the start of the war and by the time it was done, we were as close as brothers."

"My Pa always said that war was nothing but a waste of life."

"He was right about that, but it's a dang good way to judge the character of a man."

"Who was Tommy?" Digger asked, surprised that he'd never heard Heck mention his name.

"I reckon we've chewed the fat enough for a while, sonny. It's best to let the dead stay buried." Cradling his Sharps rifle in his arms, August looked out the window and saw several riders approaching from the east.

"Is that them?" Digger asked.

"It sure is, boy. You best hold on, cause things are about to get a might bumpy."

"Is everyone in place?" Red asked, as Jim sat down in the chair next to him. He had chosen the boardwalk in front of the Dancing Sow to make his stand, figuring that if it was time for him to meet his maker, it might as well be in front of his new saloon.

"They're as ready as they're gonna get, I reckon," Jim said. "August and Digger are at the hotel and Jefferson and Darby are up on the roof of the livery. Everyone else in town with any sense is hiding in their homes."

Pulling out his pocket watch, Red checked the time, which showed to be just ten minutes later than the last time he had looked. "Our guests should be arriving soon, and I want to be sure we give them a proper greeting."

"Are you sure that Lorde's men will be coming here? We may be doing all this for nothing."

"They wanted Heck out of town, so they could divide his forces. Lorde would believe that with Heck gone, the rest would be lambs to the slaughter. Mason Lorde was an Army officer and dividing your enemy's forces is a basic military tactic."

"How is that you know about military tactics?" Jim asked. Every time he thought he knew Red, he learned something else about the man. Like the gambler he was, Red always had a surprise up his sleeve.

"I wasn't always the man of questionable character that you know today. Once upon a time, I was quite respectable."

"I just hope that your men hold up their end, or Heck will be riding into a pack of trouble."

"My men are loyal, and completely reliable," Red said, slightly offended that Jim would question his judgment.

"I wish I had known you had your own army," Jim replied, shaking his head. "We could have used them when we had that trouble in Oro City."

"They've been down in Mexico for the last ten years protecting my interests there. I just wired them to come here when we heard Heck was in trouble. Knowing him like I do, I assumed we would have need of their assistance sooner or later."

"Maybe you should have had some of them come here to help us out. We're liable to have our hands full shortly."

Red waved off Jim's concern and said, "Not to worry, we will dispose of that rabble in no time."

"I hope you're right," Jim said, "cause Jefferson is signaling that we got riders approaching."

Red looked up and saw Jefferson waving his arms and pointing toward the east. He checked the loads in both of his pistols and said, "Unless Jefferson is being attacked by bees, it looks like we are about to go to work. The drinks are on me when this thing is over."

"I'll hold ya to that," Jim replied, checking his own guns.

"How is it that we got stuck on top of a roof while everyone else is all comfortable and under cover?" Darby said, wiping the sweat from his brow.

"I suppose they figure a couple of dead shots like us should be out in the open where we can do the most damage," Jefferson replied.

"Maybe they just put us up here to draw fire, so they'll have an easier time of it. They probably figure we can't get the job done, so why not have us out here to draw fire. I've heard Heck talk about them and they've killed a lot of men."

"I believe that," Jefferson said, "especially about Red."

"You don't like 'em? They seem like good men."

"Oh, I reckon they're alright. August and Jim seem like a decent sort, but I don't trust Red. He makes his fortune by taking the hard-earned money of working folk, and I figure he'd steal from his own mother."

"As long as he holds up his end in this fight, I don't care what kind of man he is," Digger said, looking down the long street.

"Maybe so," Jefferson said, "but I just hope when this is all over, we can get back to the business of ranching. Trouble just seems to follow these men."

"Speaking of trouble," Darby said, "we've got some riding into town now, and it don't look like they're here for a church social. You'd better give Red the signal."

Stepping to the edge of the roof, Jefferson waved his arms as Red had instructed him. He and Darby then stretched out on the roof and prepared for what was to come.

Chapter Thirty-Three

"Alright, sonny, this thing's gonna kick off fast, and we're only gonna get a few shots off before them devils hit the dirt," August said, as he lined up the lead rider in the sites of his Sharps.

August took his time, allowing for the wind, before his finger squeezed the trigger on the fifty-caliber. The shot lifted the man off his horse and sent him sprawling onto the dirt road.

Digger took August's place. Bringing the Winchester to his shoulder, he levered and fired five quick shots, two of which struck home, sending more of Lorde's men to the hereafter.

From the prone position, Jefferson and Darby opened fire with their rifles. Neither man could tell whose shots hit their mark, but five of the riders fell to the ground. Several of them were alive enough to make it to their feet and dash for cover, but one of them only made it a few feet before Jefferson dropped him with a shot to the back.

The rest of the invaders, seeing the futility of riding through the deadly rifle fire, leapt from their horses and dove for cover. Two made the poor decision of trying to shoot it out from behind a buckboard, which enabled the riflemen on both sides of the street to get them in a crossfire. The pair traded shots with the defenders for a few moments before being riddled with rifle bullets. Their efforts were completely in vain, as the pistols they used were not meant for a long-distance battle.

After seeing so many of their friends lying dead in the street, a few of the cowboys figured their best chance for survival was to beat a hasty retreat, so they used a lull in the shooting to make a run for the town limits.

"A few of 'em are high tailing it and the rest are digging in," Jefferson said. "We best get down there and help them boys out."

"Alright," Darby said, "but we've been having all the fun. It's time Red and Jim got in on the action."

"This might be more than they can handle. Besides, I want this cleaned up and over with."

"It would appear that August and Jefferson have done all they can do, so it is up to you and I to finish this," Red said, walking into the street. "You take the left, while I go right. Together, we will sweep up the rubbish and end this nasty business."

Jim King walked down the street, keeping to the boardwalk. He stayed close to the buildings and kept a sharp eye out for his enemy.

Forgotten Country   John Spiars

After the echo of the gunfire had died down, the town seemed very quiet and Jim imagined he could hear the slightest sound. He spun around upon hearing a loud crash, but a closer look showed it was nothing more than a couple of cats digging through a trash can.

He worked the hammer of his Smith and Wesson back and forth, just to make sure the action was functioning properly. It was an unnecessary precaution, as he always took care to make sure his guns were in working order. He did this as a ritual before every fight due to a recurring nightmare he had. It was always the same. He would be in a shooting war with an unseen enemy, but at the moment of truth, his gun would jam and he'd be killed. Jim didn't really see the point in these dreams, but he realized it must be due to a fear he carried about being at the mercy of his enemies.

Focusing on the present, Jim peered around the corner into an alley, but seeing no place for a man to hide, he continued walking down the boardwalk. The air was very still with not the slightest breath of wind, and while autumn was on the horizon, the day was going to be a Texas scorcher. Jim pulled off his coat and laid it on one of the chairs that lined the boardwalk in an effort to both stay cool and to give himself more freedom of movement.

He walked up to the window of the bakery and pressed his face to the glass. Most mornings, the smell of hot bread and sweet rolls lured the citizens of Weatherford to its doors, but this morning, the building was empty, and the ovens were not burning.

Backing away from the window, Jim caught the reflection of two men coming up behind him. One carried a machete and the other a hatchet, and they might have succeeded in cutting him to pieces if Jim hadn't stopped at the bakery window.

Jim spun around, and without raising his pistol, he drove a bullet into the temple of Zeke Slater. As Devlin watched his brother fall to the ground with blood pouring from his dead, he lunged at Jim. The blade of his machete sliced into Jim's arm, but it was only a glancing blow and did only minor damage.

Jim King grabbed the hatchet with his left hand, fending off another blow as he struggled to get the big man off of him. The two were locked in a test of strength, neither able to gain an advantage over the other as they danced first one way and then the other.

"I'm gonna cut you up slow," Devlin Slater said, his face only inches away from Jim's. "You're gonna taste some real pain before ya die." With the grunt of a wild animal, the killer worked up all the strength he could and shoved Jim backwards into the door of the bakery. Freeing his hand, he drew back the hatchet and aimed it at Jim's head, but a sudden burning in his gut caused him to drop his weapon and fall to his knees.

Devlin Slater didn't hear the shots, but looking down at his stomach, he saw that the front of his shirt was turning red with the blood that poured from two bullet holes. He gasped several times, trying to get a breath, but he couldn't seem to take in any air. The pain made him want to cry out, but just as he couldn't take in any air, he also couldn't seem to utter a sound.

"You'll be dead soon," Jim said, looking down on the man, "but until then, you should look at the pain you're in as a sample of what you'll be feeling when you get to hell."

With blood oozing from his mouth, Devlin tried to speak, but the words stuck in his throat, and after coughing twice, he fell over sideways and started his journey down below.

"Damn you, mister," Cain Slater said, stepping in front of Jim with a shotgun. "I don't know who you are, but I'm gonna enjoy killing you." Looking down at the bodies of his brothers, he wiped a tear from his cheek. "They weren't worth a darn, but they were my family and they will be revenged."

Jim looked at the two shotgun barrels pointed at his chest and knew he would never get off a shot before the scatter gun did its work on him, but he figured he had fair odds of killing the man before he died. It wasn't what he would call the best outcome, but at least he would go out fighting and perhaps take another of the Slater brothers with him. Killing three brothers in the same fight, maybe they would put that on his tombstone, he thought.

As Jim began to raise his pistol to take a shot, a loud crack echoed through downtown, and he watched as Cain Slater pitched forward and hit the ground. A hole the size of a silver dollar was torn into the man's back and the ground beneath him ran red with his blood.

Shading his eyes from the morning sun, Jim gazed down the street and saw August walking towards him, his Sharps rifle still smoking.

"Dang it, Jim," August called. "I ain't always gonna be around to save your bacon, so you need to learn to be more careful."

"I won't do any such thing," Jim replied. "Giving you the satisfaction of saving me is what keeps you young and kicking. I reckon you've got at least a few more good years left in ya anyhow."

Forgotten Country   John Spiars

Hearing four pistol shots followed by a rifle shot, the two men turned their heads and looked down the opposite end of the street.

Red stepped over the bodies of the dead, nudging them with his foot to check for signs of life. Seeing that each had already passed on to their reward, or more likely to their punishment, he moved down the street. With a Colt in each hand, Red walked in the middle of the street, watching both sides at once, and ready to act no matter which direction the attack came from.

A lifetime spent betting other men out of their money had made him rich, but it certainly wasn't without its dangers. He had never cheated anyone, but some men took losing their hard-earned money very personally, even if the game was fair. Red had made many enemies and as a result, he had developed a heightened sense of self preservation, and an almost supernatural ability to see danger before it happened.

All of his senses sought out the smallest movement or slightest sound, but as he passed in front of the bank, he began to think that anyone still alive had already made their way out of town. This thought, however, was quickly dispelled with the sound of gunfire coming from the other end of the street.

"It would appear that Jim found at least one intrepid soul with a little courage," Red whispered to himself.

He had almost decided to abandon his search in favor of lending Jim a hand when the sound of footsteps from behind caused him to wheel around.

The split second between turning and firing showed him that the man was Heck's brother Jefferson, and Red was glad he wasn't one to panic in fight.

The two men stared at each other for a moment, as if confirming that the other was indeed a friend and not one of the gunmen they sought.

"Where are all of the others?" Jefferson asked, lowering his rifle. "Are they—"

Before he could finish his thought, he saw Red extend a nickel-plated Colt. Using the palm of his left hand, Red fanned four shots directly at Jefferson, but as he looked down, instead of seeing the blood he expected, he saw that not one of the bullets had struck him.

"What are you trying to do?" Jefferson exclaimed, after double-checking that he was indeed still alive.

Red opened the loading gate of his Colt and began ejecting the spent cartridges. As he did so, he pointed with his chin, indicating that Jefferson should look behind him.

Turning around, Jefferson saw the body of Otis Lorde still clutching his cocked pistol. All four of Red's shots had hit almost on top of each other, creating one massive wound in the center of the man's chest.

Jim stared at the body of the dead marshal, not sorry that the man was dead, but trying to come to terms with how close to death he had actually been.

"Thanks," Jefferson said. He knew he should have said more, but at the moment, it was the best he could manage.

"It was my pleasure. I owe your brother my life, and that debt extends to his family as well."

"Heck sees things a bit differently. He says that it's you that saved him, but either way, I'm much obliged."

Red went back to thumbing fresh cartridges into his gun, thinking about Jefferson's words. "I suppose after all of these years, it may be that we have come to each other's aid so many times that we've lost count."

"Maybe you should both stop trying to keep count."

"Perhaps so. Let's go see if the others need our help. It's too quiet down there."

As he turned around, Red saw that a cowboy had him lined up in his rifle sites. With a smile, he waited for the inevitable blast and the death that was sure to follow.

"You should have made sure I was dead, mister," the cowboy yelled.

The cowboy had given into the sin of pride, which wasn't only against God's law, but went against the law of warfare. Instead of taking the opportunity to kill his enemy, he had felt the need to brag a little first, and it would be the last mistake he would ever make. Two rounds from Jefferson's Winchester lifted the man off his feet and onto his back. His eyes gazed into the sun, but they no longer saw anything.

"He looks dead now, don't he?" Jefferson said mockingly.

"He certainly does," Red replied. "Let's hope that he is the last of his kind infesting this town. The charm of today's activities has begun to wear thin."

"You boys still alive?" Jim called from down the street. "We heard all the shooting and thought maybe you had run into somebody you had cheated at the card table."

"I will take these aspersions directed at my character in the jovial spirit in which I'm sure they were intended, though I've certainly ended men for less."

"You won't find me as easy to kill as these drunks you're used to facing, so let's just call it a day. Besides, I've already killed my limit for one day."

"Will you two stop your dang foolishness. We're all still alive, and I believe Red owes us all a few drinks in that new saloon of his," August said.

"That sounds mighty good to me," said Digger. "I could use a whiskey or two."

"The boy will have a Sarsaparilla," Darby said, walking down the street to join the group. "Heck didn't save that boy so he could become some shiftless drunk."

"I take offense to that, young fella," August said. "My friends and me are hardly shiftless. We're honest drunks."

"Let's take this conversation to the more comfortable confines of the Dancing Sow," Red said, wiping the sweat from his brow. "With the heat, this whole affair is beginning to take on the air of actual work."

"Who's gonna clean up this mess?" Digger asked, looking at the bullet ridden buildings and the street which was littered with the bodies of the dead.

"Well, Heck's the sheriff, so I reckon that's his job," August said with a chuckle.

Chapter Thirty-Four

"I think you're making the wrong play," Red said, as he and Heck looked down on Mason Lorde's ranch house. "Let me and my men ride down there and really put an end to this whole thing."

"No," Heck replied. "I'm the sheriff and I intend to handle this according to the law. That means I take Mason Lorde alive so that he can face justice in front of a judge. Your men are here to keep Lorde from getting nervy and trying to make a fight."

"Suit yourself, but experience has taught me that when you put your hope in the law, you should be prepared for a disappointment."

"That's a pretty gloomy way to look at the law," Heck said. "This nation was built on law and order and one day the frontier will be settled because of the law."

"The law is all well and good, but the courts are controlled by money and politicians and Mason Lorde has plenty of both in his pocket."

"That's not my concern. My job is to place him in jail, and that's what I intend to do."

With Jean Waubach leading the small army, Heck and Red rode past massive herds of cattle, through the first gate, and up to the palatial home of Mason Lorde. As they rode up the long drive, Lorde's men started exiting the bunk houses to see what the commotion was all about.

The cowboys stood along the fence that led from the bunkhouse to the main house, and each brought with them every gun they owned. Most carried a rifle and wore one or two pistols on their side, though a few also held shotguns. They looked sternly at those they considered invaders on their land, but the sight of twelve heavily armed men kept them from making any moves that might lead to a shooting fight.

"Keep your men here," Heck said when they were less than a hundred feet from the house. "I'll ride the rest of the way alone. I doubt any of 'em will try anything but be ready just in case I'm wrong. I figure most of the real gun hands were sent to Ellsby and Weatherford, but these men all ride for the brand, so they're apt to follow their bosses lead."

"I'll take care of things here," Red said. "You just make sure you do the same up there."

Heck rode up to the front of the huge house and saw that Mason Lorde was standing outside, as if waiting for him. The cattle baron was not alone, a man of about forty in a finely tailored suit stood next to him.

Far from the confrontation he had expected, Heck was surprised to see that Mason Lorde greeted him with a smile on his face, as though he were actually happy to see him.

"Good evening, Sheriff Carson," the cattle baron said in a good-natured tone. "What brings you here on this fine night?"

"Mason Lorde, I have a warrant for your arrest. Judge Castleberry has ordered you to appear before him to answer charges of murder and being a general danger to the public welfare."

"Sheriff, while I can't imagine what I might have done to inspire such outrageous charges, I am more than willing to go with you to clear my good name. Let me introduce you to my attorney, Mister Junius Stillwell. He will be accompanying us as well."

"My client is innocent of these charges and is more than prepared to go before the judge to clear this matter up. I hope that the presence of so many armed men doesn't mean that you intend to go outside the bounds of the law and resort to violence. Such actions would be a clear violation of the law as well as a violation of your position as sheriff."

Heck was taken by surprise. Mason Lorde didn't seem worried about the charges he faced, in fact, he was confident and appeared to welcome the chance to have his day in court. Heck couldn't explain it, but he knew enough to be worried.

"These men are here to make sure he comes along peacefully, so as long as he keeps his men under control, he has nothing to fear, at least until he's been convicted of the charges against him. Once that happens, it will be my duty and pleasure to escort him to his hanging."

"That is one pleasure I'm afraid you'll be denied," Lorde replied, "because I have no intention of being convicted of anything. This county belongs to me, as does everything and everyone in it. You'll come to see that sooner or later."

Chapter Thirty-Five

"Good afternoon, judge. What can I do for you today?" Heck asked, walking up to the sheriff's office after making his rounds of the town.

"I wanted to tell you face to face before you heard it from someone else. All of the charges against Mason Lorde have been dropped. You are ordered to release him immediately with all apologies from the county for any inconvenience he suffered," Judge Castleberry said, unable to look Heck in the eye.

"What do ya mean turn him loose?" Heck exclaimed, not believing what he was hearing. "He ordered an attack on Ellsby and Weatherford, not to mention murdering Sheriff Garhardt. How can they just let him go?"

"His lawyer was an aid to two state senators as well as a U.S. Representative, so he's got a lot of political contacts who owe him favors. Mason Lorde also has plenty of money that he's been spreading around. It seems he's been making some big promises about how he plans to build up Parker County, and that means great wealth for those in positions of power. For some, that is far more important than seeing justice done."

"So Red was right," Heck said angrily. "Money and politics control the law and justice is lost somewhere in all the deal making."

"It's not just that, Heck. Mason Lorde claimed to know nothing about the attacks on Ellsby and Weatherford. He says that his men acted on their own because they were angry about you arresting Earl Mosby, and he had nothing to do with it. He even denounced his own brother as a crooked sheriff who was so mad about losing the election that he planned the whole attack on Weatherford as an act of revenge. Mister Lorde also claims to be totally innocent of murdering Sheriff Garhardt. He claims it was a case of mistaken identity, and all of the witnesses have backed up his side of things. They say that it was some drunk drifter who killed the sheriff and that Lorde wasn't even in town."

"Don't you see that Lorde has gotten to them and threatened them not to tell what they saw."

"I'm sure that's true," Judge Castleberry said, "but we can't prove it. Lorde's attorney got the governor to appoint a state judge, so I was cut out of the case entirely. There are powers at work here that are more powerful than you and me, so we have no choice but to let him go free. I have my orders and now so do you. I'm sorry, Heck, but that's the way things are."

Walking in to the office, Heck was greeted by Darby who he had taken on as a sheriff's deputy.

Forgotten Country   John Spiars

"Why the long face, Heck? Don't tell me we have to appear in court again. We have both told our story. They should be able to hang Mason Lorde three times with what you and me have told them."

"We have to let him go," Heck said. "It seems he's bought his freedom with money and political connections. Judge Castleberry just told me."

"What do we do now?" Darby asked. "We can't set him free. He'll just hire more gun hands to kill us and terrorize the county."

"I know," Heck replied, "but we ain't got no choice. We represent the law, and the law is telling us to turn him loose. Give me the key. I might as well get this over with."

As Heck opened the door to his cell, Mason Lorde wore the look of a man who was completely in control. His smug look seemed to say, "What took you so long? I told you I would be set free."

He strolled out of his cell with a smile on his face, as if he knew that things would always go his way.

"Good morning. I was afraid I was going to be forced to spend another night in these deplorable accommodations. No offense, the food from the café is quite good, but the bed isn't fit for a civilized man."

"My orders were to release you from jail, but there wasn't nothing said about what condition you had to be in when I did it. Until you're out of my jail, I would advise you to keep your mouth shut, because all sorts of accidents can happen in a place like this."

"C'mon Heck, I wouldn't have pegged you as a sore loser," Mason said with the confident smile of one who always expects to win. "You and your boys did pretty well.

I mean, you all came out alive, well, except for poor Ulley that is, but I suppose ya can't win 'em all."

"Darby, give Mister Lorde back his possessions and show him out."

"Nothing is over between us, Heck," Lorde said. "You may have won a few battles, but I will win the war. You know why I'll win? I'll win because it is my destiny to win, and because I refuse to let anything, or anybody stand in my way. You and your men had better clear out or that ranch of yours will be nothing more than a handy place to bury you. You're not ranchers, anyway. You're nothing but a bunch of killers looking for a violent death, and I'm just the man to give it to ya."

"Mason, let me tell ya something. If I see you or any of your boys on my land, you're a dead man. I will come to your ranch and kill everything that walks or crawls there and then I'll burn the whole thing to the ground. I tried to leave justice to the law, but next time, I will be the one passing out justice and that is something that I am very good at. Now get out of my jail before I decide to save myself a lot of aggravation and just kill you now."

"Good day, Mister Carson," Mason said, as he walked out of the door.

"You mean Judge Castleberry just let him off?" Jefferson exclaimed.

"No, Lorde got a state judge appointed to hear the case, and he ordered me to turn him loose," Heck said, sipping from his coffee cup.

"I told you how this was going to go," Red said. He knew he shouldn't brag, but he couldn't help himself. "You should have let me and my men handle Mason Lorde.

We could have been finished with this whole matter by now and been ready to move on to the next catastrophe."

"It's too late to be thinking about what we should've done," Jim said. "I don't suppose that Mason has plans on moving out of the county now that he's been released?"

"It don't seem so," Heck said. "I figure things will go back to the way they were before, with Lorde trying to run off all of the small farmers and ranchers. Of course, I'm sure he has built up a pretty powerful hate for us, after killing his brother and most of his gunfighters. He'll be coming for us before long, so we best be prepared."

"Well, at least it'll take him some time to recruit a new army of gunhands," Jefferson said, trying to think positively.

"It won't take him that long," Red replied. "Not with his money."

"What do we do now?" Digger asked.

"We get back to the business of ranching. That's what I came here to do, and I ain't gonna be deterred by the likes of Mason Lorde. August, Jim, you boys have a home on my ranch if ya want it."

"I ain't never seen myself being no rancher," August said.

"Well, there are worse things to be," Heck said.

"I reckon you're right about that. I reckon I could give it a go."

"Me too," Jim said. "It seems that the business of law has passed me by."

"What about me?" Red asked. "Do I not get the same generous offer?"

"You're a good man, Red," Heck said, "but you're also a loafer, and I ain't looking for one of those right now. Besides, you've got a new saloon to open, don't ya?"

"That is true," Red replied. "I figure you boys will be good customers, so I will have it open for business very soon."

"What is the name of this ranch of yours?" Jim asked.

"Yeah, you've gotta give it a name," Jefferson said. "I don't intend to be a partner in some no name ranch. That would be too embarrassing."

"I've been giving that some thought, and I've decided to call it Paradise Ridge, and our brand will be the Double C."

"The Double C? For Carson?" Jefferson said.

"It will stand for something else as well," Heck said. "If I can convince her to join me here."

"I reckon Paradise Ridge is a fair name," Jefferson said. "I could be proud to ride for that brand."

"I'm glad to hear that," Heck replied, "because we've all got a lot of work ahead of us. It seems to me that the only way to beat Mason Lorde is to become richer and more powerful than he is, and that starts with the ranch. That's how we'll survive, but in the end, it'll still come down to a fight, but it's a fight we're gonna win. I promise you that."

Chapter Thirty-Six

Heck reined his horse to a stop in front of the large house on the south side of Fort Worth. Red had given him the directions, but he still wasn't sure he was at the right home. The street was lined with beautiful houses that were bigger than any he had ever seen, and he couldn't have felt any more out of place if he had been sitting in on a ladies' sewing circle.

He made his way up the cobblestone walk and looked up at the massive home which was made of brick, stone and marble. The ornate peaks and gables reminded Heck of the pictures he had seen of European castles. He was sure he must have been at the wrong house, but as the door opened, he saw the beautiful form of Caroline Farber step onto the front porch.

"Good morning, Mister Carson," she said, with a smile that immediately made Heck want to smile as well, though he wasn't sure it was necessarily evidence that she was happy to see him.

"Good morning, ma'am," Heck replied. Upon seeing her, Heck felt the old nervousness returning. It was a feeling he could never quite explain, as it only seemed to happen in her presence.

As he drew closer to Caroline, a light breeze carried the faint scent of lilies and cherry blossoms, the smell of which Heck associated with the only woman that he had ever truly loved. The silk and ruffles of Caroline's green dress rustled as she stepped off the wooden porch to greet Heck. If he had to name a moment above all others where he knew he would do anything for the woman, it would have been right then on the porch of that huge house.

"That's a beautiful house you've got yourself," Heck said. "I leave you alone for a few weeks and you become the cattle queen of Texas."

"I don't appreciate you making fun of me, Mister Carson. You know very well that this house belongs to your friend, Mister Tillerson. He just thought that since he wasn't using it presently, that I might be more comfortable here than in the room above the saloon, especially since whatever danger I was in seems to have passed."

"Red certainly does know how to live, I'll say that."

"What brings you here, Mister Carson?" she asked, pacing up and down the walk. "If you just came to check on me, you needn't have bothered. As you can see, I am doing just fine. If you came here because you think your friend might be courting me, you can turn around and leave, because that, sir, is none of your business."

"You used to call me Jesse, but now it's Mister Carson. Why the change, Caroline?" Heck asked, stopping her and putting his hands on her shoulders.

Pulling away from his grasp, Caroline walked back onto the porch, as if to go inside the house, but she suddenly stopped and turned back around. "We were going somewhere then. We had a future, but then you left in pursuit of something, something that I couldn't offer. It was then that I knew that marriage would be a prison for you, and no matter what I did, it couldn't compare to the life on the trail that you love so much. I refuse to take second place to anything or anyone."

"I'm sorry that you felt that way, Caroline, but I only left because I couldn't give you the life you deserved. I needed to earn more money to start my ranch, and to build a life that would be worthy of you. You deserve a better life than that of being married to a town marshal. I was trying to build a future for us, a future that is within our grasp now. I am building a ranch that will allow me to give you all that you deserve, and all that is missing is you to share it with."

"I read the newspaper, Jesse. I know what happened in Ellsby and Weatherford, and it's not the life I want. I don't want a man who is consumed with ugliness and death. I want a husband and children. I want a family, Jesse, not a man who just moves from one war to another."

"I am trying, Caroline. I will resign as sheriff and devote my time to the ranch and that family you speak of. I want to marry you."

Taking Heck's hand, Caroline looked into his eyes, "I don't care if you're a rancher or a sheriff, that's not what matters to me. I just want you to be devoted to me and the children we would have, not to some dream of adventure that you're still holding onto. I want you to be devoted to me, just as I would be devoted to you."

"I will be devoted to you for all of my days, but I want a good life for us and our family, and I will not stop until I achieve that. I want you to come back to Weatherford with me, and I want us to be married as soon as you think it's proper. I want you to see Paradise Ridge, our ranch, and I want you to pick out the best spot for our house. That is what I want. That is what I'm offering. What do you say, Caroline?"

"What do I say? I say, you had better be sure, because I'm not one to let a man go back on his promise."

"I never go back on my promises," Heck said, "and I will love you for the rest of my life."

"In that case," Caroline said, "why don't you show me this ranch of ours."

Heck took Caroline in his arms and kissed her, knowing that from that moment on, he would never let her go.

ABOUT THE AUTHOR

JOHN SPIARS is a western writer and amateur historian with a passion for telling the stories of the American West. He lives in North Texas with his wife and four children. When not writing novels, he maintains a website dedicated to Texas history and travel and a Facebook Page: Under the Lone Star.

CONNECT ONLINE

underthelonestar.com

OTHER BOOKS BY JOHN SPIARS:

Riders of the Lone Star: Heck Carson Series Volume 1

Hell and Half of Texas: Heck Carson Series Volume 2

Bound for Vengeance: Heck Carson Series Volume 3

Blood Trail: Heck Carson Series Volume 4

Last Stand at Paradise Ridge: Heck Carson Series Volume 6

Bury me at Palmetto Creek

Made in the USA
Coppell, TX
26 November 2023